The Blood Covenant: Mistrust, Division, & Murder

Kornelia Blackmore

Published by Kornelia Blackmore, 2021.

THE BLOOD COVENANT: MISTRUST, DIVISION, & MURDER

First edition. October 31, 2021.

Copyright © 2021 Kornelia Blackmore.

ISBN: 978-1735307206

Written by Kornelia Blackmore.

Dedication

This book (although fiction) is based on the power of our (subconscious) covenant with fear.

Our inherent beliefs that were taught to us by our ancestors (which is the generational curse of hatred as a child). Is what perpetuates everyone's cycle of suffering and creates Act One: Mistrust of everyone that is not, or does not look like us.

Our generational curses are what keeps us in Act Two: Divided into believing that it is my beliefs, thoughts, and feelings against yours, i.e I'm right. You're wrong.

This Division is what what causes wars, violence, bloodshed and ultimately Act Three: Murder (Blood).

Our subconscious Covenant with fear is why we all pay the ultimate price, and that's bloodshed.

Welcome to The Blood Covenant.

The moral of this story, is to challenge your own beliefs, take a step back, and ask questions.

Never stop asking, because when we ask questions about ourselves and the world around us, that's how we all conquer our fears and unite as the human race.

This message came to me in a nightmare I experienced back in September of 2021, it was so vivid I wrote down the outline and the rest I filled in the blanks.

Remember, I love you, so don't give up the fight, don't run, and face your own demons. You're a helluva lot tougher than you give yourself credit for.
-Kornelia Blackmore

Act 1: Mistrust
Chapter 1: Generational Curses
Tessa (Red) Parker

So there's this school (a community college) that I go to, and it's like the air here is so thick with tension you could cut the shit with a knife. Literally, it feels like a fight could break out at any moment, and it didn't matter where it was taking place, be it inside the dingy brick (lumpy walled) building with dull grey floors or outside on the cloudy winter day.

I was walking towards the science building in the back behind the main campus, and when the cold wind nipped at my cheeks, I was reminded of how poor I am, cuz it may snow, and I got no damn gloves or socks to afford this fucking weather. Go figure.

I caught sight of one of my classmates, Inessa, whose a girl I met from my English Comp class. She's from Russia but came to the states to get her degree in the medical field, but since there's like a million majors in the medical field, I honestly couldn't remember; I have shitty memory for most things, and I know I gotta get better with it.

"Hey, girl!" I waved to her, and when her blue eyes met mine, she grinned.

"Hello!" She replied, stopping for a sec to hug me in the middle of the cobblestone walkway, and I inhaled her shampoo, which smelled fresh instead of flowery like most girly shampoos. It's why I love her as much as I do.

She broke from our embrace and flipped her long wavy blonde hair over her green coat with a smile, then gripped the straps of her book bag.

Even though she's smiling, the light form of wrinkles on her forehead told me otherwise (even though she's still like twenty-something).

I'm telling you, this girl is like always stressed the fuck out, and yes, I'm the one that reminds her to chill cuz she's super high-strung and nervous. But it's why I adore her.

"Which class you headed to?" I asked.

"I headed to Anatomy, text me?" she said in her thick Russian accent, bolting past me to the blue-colored double doors behind, "Kay! Laters!" I shouted, and she waved back at me.

It sucks she gets picked on by the other students cuz they don't understand her accent, but I don't judge at all; I don't see why. Or what the point is, really.

I stuffed my hands in the pockets of my hoodie and continued to walk to my science class.

WHEN I STEPPED INTO the classroom, the industrial lights above were super fucking bright today, and it made my heart sink to the pits, beat against my chest & made my stomach clench at the same time, which is my intuition screaming at me that some shit is about to pop off. No, I'm just making this shit up again; I immediately dismissed and plopped my shit down on the big black table.

The guys were dickin around talking shit, and the other girls settled into their respective cliques as the rest of the students shuffled into class & the plump dude with balding gray hair was writing some shit on the chalkboard.

"Hey boo," Kalina (Fox) mentioned & I shook my head to come back to center and dismiss that feeling I had.

"Sis, you good? You look pale as fuck," she asked, rubbing my back & I took a deep breath to calm my hands trembling. What the fuck? So I took another deep breath, "Yeah, I'm good, just my brain fucking with me again."

"Hey, it's all good, listen this school is so goddamn stressful, so I don't blame you, and sis not to make your anxiety worse, but I gotta letchu know, did you hear about the shootout that happened around the apartment complex next to the school last night? Apparently, it was between Lamar, and Peter & both of them are dead," She shifted in her seat to give me her full attention.

I paled as the incident flashed in my mind when she told me, see, I'm spiritually sensitive, but I don't say shit to nobody:

Lamar: Ayo, you fuckin my girl! He shouted where he stood outside the apartment complex in the parking lot with a row of cars behind him.

Peter: So what! Fuck you! The dude shouted back where he marched towards him while pulling out his pistol & aimed it at Lamar, and he did the same.

Bang! Bang! Bang! Bang! Bang! And in a flash, I saw both of their carcasses laying slump on the parking lot with both of their thick blood mixing and flowing down the drain.

"Settle down, guys!" Mr. Oscar commented, and it broke me from my thoughts. He said it with no conviction at all, and I don't blame him, cuz we grown and my classmates don't listen worth a damn.

"Girl, no, I didn't hear about that shit!" I replied, trying to shake off the image I saw, hoping I wasn't right, but I'm pretty sure I am right. And it sucks being right.

"Yup, turns out Peter was fuckin Lamar's girl, and now she's devastated she lost both, girl, what the fuck is this world coming to?" Kalina (who me I call Fox) said with disappointment.

Son of a bitch, I thought, gritting my teeth & tried to erase it.

I grabbed my iPhone from my pocket & noticed I had a group text from Inessa (who I also call Stone, or Nessa, depending): "We carpool together later? Lmk, bye!" She's so adorable.

Fox checked her phone, and she texted to both of us, "Yup, I'm Gucci, sis," and I replied to the two girls, "Yup, we're using my car," Nessa texted & thank God. I was not trying to take the bus home today.

"I need you all to turn in your assignments from last night, make sure to leave the paper on my desk," Mr. Oscar said.

We both locked our phones and resumed class together.

WHEN WE LEFT FOR THE day, I kept getting all these tense, weird stares from everyone, and it made me even more unsettled, and the longer the day dragged on, the harder it became to ignore it.

"Excuse me! I need to see your student ID!" The black security officer said when me and Fox tried to enter the cafeteria to meet up with Nessa.

"Oh shit yeah, sorry," I said with a giggle to try and lighten the mood while reaching for my wallet in my backpack, "You think this shit is funny?" He snapped, getting for the taser on his hip and held it.

I glared at him, confused. Why was he so upset with me laughing? What the fuck is wrong with these people today?

"Hey, hey, I'm sorry, you're right. This is serious, my bad," I immediately apologized.

The other students who were in line to get into the cafeteria groaned behind me & Fox showed him her ID, "Excuse me, don't you think you're a little excessive?" She claimed, putting her Student ID back into her wallet.

"I'm gonna need to search your bag, miss," He demanded.

I offered it to him, he's not gonna find anything in it cuz I know better than to carry (evident) weapons in it.

He snatched it and pulled all my shit out, went through my folders, crumpled up my papers, and legit searched me like I stole money from him. What the hell is wrong with people? Why is everyone so on edge? I thought, trying to calm myself down, cuz I could feel my anger boiling the longer he kept going through my stuff.

He even searched my wallet and found my student ID, scanned it, and then tossed all my shit haphazardly inside my backpack.

"Thank you; you can go now," He snarled as I took my bag from him and slung it around my shoulder.

I knew Fox was about to say something, but I grabbed her wrist to calm her down as my way of telling her don't say anything.

I took another deep breath and plastered a smile on my face, "Thank you, have an awesome day," I said, dragging Fox with me into the dilapidated cafeteria lined with dark blue walls and rows of tables.

When I turned to look behind me, I noticed he didn't give any of the other black students a problem like he just did with me. God, he's why I hate people.

Nessa had reserved us a table, and I smiled and waved, "Can you believe that fucking asshole? Like where the fuck does he get off thinking he could just do or say some shit like that!" Fox complained.

"What happened?" Nessa asked when we both sat down at the cafeteria table, ignoring the mindless chatter of the other students, laughing, jeering and whatever the fuck else. It sounded like a goddamn zoo to me.

"Sis, the fucking security officer was about to TAZE Red!" She said.

We all have our nicknames, and even though we've only known each other for a few months, we just all clicked.

"Eh, it's not uncommon where I'm from," Nessa replied casually with a shrug while eating her home-packed lunch.

Fox grabbed her bag and pulled out a bobby pin to put up her half-shaved long pink hair away from her face, "Well fuck that this is AMERICA we don't do shit like that out here!" She barked.

"Damn, Moscow sounds fucked up," I said to her while looking for my credit card to buy lunch, and she laughed, "You should hear how bad it was during the pandemic."

"This world is so fucked up. I swear it's why I hate this shit," Fox rolled her eyes.

The reason we call her Fox is cuz she's one of them gorgeous Japanese American girls. Who happens to be mixed with black. So it's like she's got the curvy body of a black girl, dresses like a sexy Goth with all kinda tattoos & piercings, has the attitude of a black girl, and the smarts of an Asian.

Nessa, on the other hand, is more traditional and reserved until you give her a couple sips of wine & she cuts loose, we even taught her how to twerk, and I'm never deleting that video ever. Slender curvy (cuz she got a boob job done for her husband in the military) with a thick Russian accent, long blonde hair & bright blue eyes that could easily compete with the top models in America. But she doesn't think so & it kills Fox and me to no end.

Me and Fox sat up from the cafeteria table and walked through the bustling crowd of students taunting and jeering each other only to notice the way they were avoiding me and Fox, "high yella bitch," I heard one girl snicker. "Redbone," I heard another peer group tease.

"The fuck did you say?!" Fox shouted, and I stopped her cuz I knew they were talking about me, and for some reason, the air is oddly thick with tension. Something's not right.

Then boom, a fight broke out right in front of me, and without warning, I grabbed Fox and stepped in front to shield her from the dude in front about to hit another dude.

"Ayo! You bumped into me first!"

"Fuck you!" One black kid shouted to the white kid, and blows were exchanged before security was called and pulled them off of each other. I looked around, and all of them were glaring at ME like I somehow started the fight between them.

"Sis, let go. I'm fine," Fox whispered, but I felt her tremble behind me, so I didn't budge.

"It's cool," I told her despite the way my stomach clenched at this whole thing. I'm too fucking scared myself, but I can't think about that right now.

"What happened!" Nessa said where she stood beside me, "Not right now, later, let's get the fuck outta here. Get our shit Nessa, and we gotta go,"

"But fuck that! I'm hungry!" Fox whined, and I lightly pressed my heel on the toe of her boots, "OW, what the fuck!"

"HEY! Where do you think you're going!" The same fucking security officer shouted, "Fox, take Nessa and get out the cafe, do what I said now," I instructed, "Don't ask questions, just go now," I told her as calmly as I could manage while the security officer was storming towards me, but right now I'm sweating mad bullets.

"I'm not leaving you," Fox kept arguing, "Fox let's go, now!" Nessa said, yanking Fox away from my back, where she hid behind.

When I heard them hurry away, the security officer stepped to me, "Oh, you are on a fucking roll today, missy, first you try to laugh like this shit is funny, what not gonna laugh now?!" He shouted.

I stood my ground firmly and tried to shake the tension from my hands, and the heat that blasted from above only made the sweat drip down my brow, then I dry swallowed my spit.

"Nah, not really, listen if I started this or caused any problems, I'm sorry," I immediately apologized, raising my hands; the last thing I need is to piss this guy off anymore cuz he's got a weapon, and I don't since they took all my shit with them. I peeped from the corner of my eye that there were plastic forks and knives and made a mental note. Since the students were gathering around, they laughed at me, causing my heart to sink to the pits. What the fuck is happening? This isn't the same school, is it?

I can't say why I told them to leave. It was just something I knew I had to tell them so I wouldn't drag them in my shit. They don't deserve that, not when they've been the only real friends I've had in all of ever.

"You're lucky I didn't find any weapons; otherwise, I'd have to arrest you, and judging from the way you're standing there, this fight is your fault. What did you see?"

"I didn't see anything. I was just walking to go and get some food, and when I tried to walk through the crowd, some dudes said some shit, and then next thing I knew, they were throwing hands at each other; seriously, I have no idea what the hell is happening anymore," I said honestly, maybe if I show him how scared I am, he might back off.

Deciding that would be the best course of action instead of trying not to look scared like I've always done, even when I am, I let my raised hands tremble slightly, and when he saw it, "Look, get the fuck outta here before I have to arrest you," he accused. Usually, I would challenge it, but now is not the time.

"Thank you, officer, and seriously, I am so sorry,"

"You're dismissed," He barked.

I calmly walked towards the door as the crowd parted for me, and as soon as I looked over my shoulder and saw the group surround the two boys, I bolted for the door. Normally I wouldn't run, but something is wrong. I couldn't put my finger on it, but my heart was racing, my palms were sweaty, and hell, I was sweaty.

They were both waiting for me outside cuz I could see them standing through the tiny window of the double doors. So I took a deep breath to calm my shivers. Get your shit together, sis.

I straightened my back, and strolled through the doors and was met with the brisk cold wind. Goddammit, I should've been bought some fuckin gloves.

"What the hell was all that about?" Fox argued, "Look, I didn't need you guys caught up in whatever the fuck just happened," I explained.

"She's right," Nessa agreed with me, and it made me really wonder if the shit she's been through living in Russia is the reason she's as solid as she is, but it would make sense; her husband is in the military, and its fucking Moscow. Of course, she would be a tough bitch.

"Well, what the fuck ever dude, can we just go? Please?" She begged me, "Yeah, let's get outta here and go and get some real food," Nessa smiled, handing us our stuff back, and I slung my backpack over my shoulder; then I took another breath "Yeah, sounds good, sis." I said, walking with them towards Nessa's car since I felt more comfortable driving her SUV.

Chapter 2: Survival Mode
Tessa (Red) Parker

For some reason, the GPS told us to make a left on a street I did not recognize, having us take the back way behind the woods with lots of trees and shit, and it made me unsettled. It was like my heart was racing and sank to the pit of my stomach at the same time.

My instincts are screaming at me that something was really wrong, cuz it suddenly went pitch black the longer we drove, and the street became more and more narrow; I noticed clutching the steering wheel tight enough till my knuckles were white.

"Hey, sis, where the fuck are we going?" I heard Fox say from the backseat as she hovered over my neck, "We must be taking a detour," I said, doing what I could to remain calm, but something was REALLY wrong. No, it's okay, calm down, it's just my mind getting ahead of me, I thought to myself. I'm just making shit up again. It has to be my illness or some shit, yeah right, okay, that's why.

"Though I've never been down this road before, in fact, I've never seen it," Nessa brought to my attention as if confirming my original thought to be scared out my fucking mind. But when I turned to face her in the passenger side, she had a stern expression on her face, as if she knew something I didn't know.

"Oh my God, please just get us the fuck outta here," Fox kept saying over and over, "Seriously, this shit isn't funny, guys! Get us back on the main road," She kept demanding.

"Quiet," Nessa said to her calmly, and thank God, cuz I cannot handle her being erratic right now, cuz she's gripping the damn headrest so tight I can feel her panic from behind me.

"Will all of you just please calm down," I reminded, dry swallowing my spit. Goddamn, I need some fucking water, and I haven't eaten shit since this morning when I had toast for breakfast.

So I kept driving through the windy road, and then the GPS said, "Turn left," and I decided to stop while all of us looked down the rocky dirt path that led into the woods.

"Oh no, fuck that GPS, we are NOT going down that road, somethin is up with that damn GPS, and it's trying to get us murdered out here,"

"Will you please shut the fuck up!" I snapped, and cuz my hands were so sweaty, I did all I could to calm my racing heart and my stomach clenching and ignore the growling at the same goddamn time. Son of a bitch.

"We have no choice,"

Then a horn honked from behind us, and since it's a one-way street, I turned down the road, and the car rocked when we turned into the woods. What the fuck is happening? Someone, please tell me this shit is not happening.

Since the window was open, I heard some type of chanting and shouting from the car behind us, "SIS! THAT GODDAMN CAR IS FOLLOWING US!!" Fox shouted.

"WHAT!" I argued, and Nessa stayed eerily calm, "What do they want?" Fox asked, and I could hear the shiver in her voice like she was on the verge of tears.

"They're probably trying to get back to the main road like us," Nessa suggested, and I looked at her again, and she kept her eyes level on the road ahead of us, thank you for being Stone right now and not Nessa. I needed it more than I cared to let her know right now.

But when bullets started to rattle and ricochet off the frame of the SUV, Fox screamed, "GET DOWN!" I shouted, and they did as I kept driving faster and faster until the trees whizzed by, and it was like the trees were closing in on us the faster we went.

"SIS, I'M NOT READY TO DIE! OH GOD, PLEASE!"

"FOX, SHUT UP!" I shouted, and a bullet went through the windshield and cracked the front, "Great, how am I supposed to explain to my husband how his care got messed up!?" Nessa commented where she curled into a ball on the floor by the passenger seat.

"GODDAMMIT, STONE!" I shouted, and she started laughing, "WHAT THE FUCK IS WRONG WITH YOU!" Fox screeched, having a full-on meltdown. And then there were more chanting and bullets fired from the car pursuing us as the vehicle kept rocking and bouncing the faster we drove, "Well, I don't know about you, but this situation has officially gone to shit," Nessa said calmly.

Then I decided to slam my foot on the breaks to make them stop, and the front of the car rammed the butt of the car hard enough for us to jerk forward.

"Oh my God, I'm gonna die, I'm too fucking young to die, I can't, sis, I can't get us the fuck outta here. What are you doing!"

"SAVING YOUR ASS!" I argued.

Stone kept laughing, and she reached for something under the passenger seat, rolled down the window, and pointed her small pistol out the window, "NESSA WHAT THE FUCK ARE YOU DOING!"

"I'm going to shoot them."

"OH MY GOD, PUT THE GODDAMN GUN AWAY! I KNEW YOU WERE FUCKING CRAZY FROM THE START!" Fox kept yelling.

I looked at my rearview mirror and noticed it was a group of people. However, I couldn't see cuz the smoke from their car and headlights blinded me, so I couldn't identify who they were, but one thing I could make out from their silhouette was what they were carrying; and when I realized what it was, my blood went cold.

"Maybe they just wanna talk?" Fox shivered a sob where she sat crouched behind the driver's seat; that's why she was pissed when I slammed the breaks. These people were carrying spears and guns and not the tiny kind either; it was shotguns and AK's, from what I could tell.

"Now, can I shoot them?" Nessa asked me, "Wait," I said, glaring down at my hands and noticed they were shaking violently. I let out a shuddering breath to calm myself down.

"Wait, who died and made you the fucking leader!" Fox argued with me, and they kept walking towards the car as they almost huddled around it.

"Shut up, Fox, for once, please, just stay quiet,"

"Maybe it's Park Rangers or something, and maybe they can get us the fuck outta here; I need to be around people again. I can't deal with this shit right now," she cried.

I noticed Stone hid her gun under her blouse and turned to face me with a stern expression, both of us silently acknowledging between us that Toto, we aren't in Kansas anymore.

Then a black kid who looked to be our age stepped beside the driver's seat, and I peeped from the corner of my eye. There were two people on both sides of the doors by the backseat windows, and from the rearview mirror, two more people stood behind us.

"Well, that was really rude of you to go and wreck our car like that when we were just trying to have some fun," He claimed with a friendly smile.

I chuckled wryly, "Ah right, sorry, listen; we'll find a way to pay for the damages,"

"Don't worry. You won't get very far, not from us anyway,"

"What do you want, you fucking psycho!" Fox shouted from the backseat.

"Oh, didn't you know? These woods are hunting grounds, and what better target practice than you guys, seeing as you're lost and all,"

"No, no, we aren't lost, really, just uh, we took a detour to get to the main road back to the city," I lied, but when the guy looked at my hands gripping the steering wheel tight, and my heart was beating so damn loud it rang in my ears, please I hope he can't hear my heart racing like a fucking jackhammer.

"Oh yeah?" He said, taking his stance, and aimed the AK at me, and when he did, I held my hands up, "What the fuck is wrong with you! Someone call the goddamn police,"

"There's no signal out here, stupid!" I heard someone else shout southeast of me, and I knew this was the guy standing in front of Fox.

I'm gonna die.

We're all gonna die, all by the hands of some deranged psycho who's literally the exact fucking age as me. What the fuck? What the fuck? What the ACTUAL fuck!

"Tell you what, since this is our territory, I'll go ahead and give you a headstart—" and before I had a chance to answer, Nessa had fired her pistol, and when it did, it snapped me out of my daze, I turned the car on, shifted gears, and slammed on the gas trying to get as much distance between them and us.

I'm sweating bullets, my ears are ringing, my heart is racing, I can't see shit out here cuz it's getting dark, I'm hungry as fuck right now.

"NESSA, WHAT THE FUCK! OH MY GOD! PLEASE, SOMEONE, HELP US!" Fox kept hollering. I ignored it at this point; she's too far gone to realize how much deep shit we're in right now. This shit is going by too fucking fast; I didn't even get a complete profile of the guy before he aimed his weapon at me and was gonna fire it at us. They were all going to kill us.

Nessa kept popping off more shots from the side of the window as I kept driving, "When in Russia, this is what we do,"

"WELL, THIS IS NOT FUCKING RUSSIA, STUPID BITCH!! SOMEONE, PLEASE TELL ME THIS IS FUCKING NIGHTMARE! I WANT OUT! I WANNA GO HOME!"

"That's not gonna happen, sis," I reminded.

It was weird; the faster it all happened, the slower it all went, the sound of bullets bouncing off the car, the bang of Nessa's pistol where she pointed out the passenger window, the sound of Fox's choked sobs in full-on panic and fear, the darker the sky became the further we drove into what felt like limitless woods like there was no end or light at the end of this tunnel, I was suddenly calm.

God, if I'm meant to die in this shit, it won't be because I didn't give them a fight. I've been through too much shit in my life to let it end like this, fuck them, I thought, making up my mind to do what was necessary. Cursing myself for having to use what I thought I never had to use again, Goddammit.

"I'm out of bullets," Nessa mentioned calmly, and I knew Fox was done and was too far gone to say anything else to either of us.

"Shit," I said, slamming my hand on the steering wheel, "Goddammit,"

"Hey, we're in this now,"

"I know, Nessa, I fucking know," I panicked.

Then the car died down and came to a slow stop, and yet again, it was like someone had sucker-punched me, and I couldn't breathe all over again. Shit.

"Nessa, please tell me you have food and water in this car,"

"Of course, I never leave unprepared," She smiled as if firing a weapon at someone is totally normal. I guess in her country; it would be.

I pulled the key out of the ignition, and when I hopped out, the SUV leaves and twigs crunched under my boots and was met with cold, brittle air against my cheeks, and since I was, I shivered. Nessa walked around to me and held out her hand, "I'll hold the keys this time. We use the vehicle to camp out, yes?" She suggested. It would be a good idea.

"I'll stand guard. Whatchu got for food?" I offered.

"Mostly canned goods and beef jerky,"

"For how long?"

"Oh, I don't know a good week or so's worth,"

"You really mapped this out, didn't you,"

"When in Russia," She smiled, tucking her tiny silver pistol under her green coat and blouse.

"Guys, you aren't seriously thinking about camping out here?! How about we just go back to the main road? It's probably easier that way," Fox whined from the backseat window, too shook to move from her spot. I don't blame her one bit, but I just wish she knew when to shut up cuz her paranoia is only making this situation worse.

I strolled to the backseat where she inserted her key and popped the trunk door, then pulled back the floor where she had gallons of water stashed, towels, tools, bags of beef jerky, canned foods, and a whole lot of other shit. This should get us through for a while.

"I have blankets stashed in another compartment," She informed, "Thank you, Nessa,"

"Seriously, why can't we just walk back to the main road!?" Fox kept whining where she looked at both of us with tears coating her cheeks from the backseat, "No, too cold. You'll freeze to death, better to stay here with us,"

"She's right, Fox. It's better to stay here. Besides, who knows where those fucking psychos are, and it's better for us to stick together,"

"You guys are joking, just some elaborate prank, well you guys are just as crazy and fucked up as they are, you're—you're in on it with them, aren't you! Right, you have to be, cuz Halloween is around the corner, right? I should've known!" Fox kept accusing us.

"Izumi, do me a favor and get a fucking grip, we CAN'T go back, we CAN'T call for help, cuz there's no goddamn signal out here, and do you honestly think we would be in on some shit like this?!"

"Nessa shot at those guys! Those can't be real bullets,"

"Wanna hop out the car and find out for yourself?!"

"GUYS, STOP IT!" I shouted, "Us fighting isn't gonna solve anything; in fact, those guys WANT us to fight. Haven't any of you fucker's seen horror films before?!"

"Ah yes, I am familiar with it," Nessa said, grabbing the jug of water, popped the cap, and took a long swig, "I also have some vodka in here as well."

Good, I need it. I think we all do.

"Well, moral of the fucking story when we split up, that's when one of us dies okay! So please, Izumi, I am ASKING you to please trust us. Wasn't it me who told ya ass to roll out when that security officer was in my face for some shit I didn't do?!"

"Well, maybe it was part of it. I've only known you for a couple of months. I seriously had no idea you guys were this fucked up in the head,"

"Then leave," Nessa ordered, "You know what, maybe I will! Fuck this! I'm outta here!" Fox agreed, sliding out the backseat, slammed the door, and stormed back up the dirt road.

We both looked at each other, "Stone," I said sternly, and her firm blue eyes met mine, "What?"

I balled my hands in a fist but said nothing to her cuz right now; I'm on the verge of tears, my damn self. I'm so shook and scared out of my fuckin mind, and I can't make any more sense of this shit than Izumi can right now.

"Go apologize and bring her ass back here before those guys find her, please?" I asked.

"Why? What for? She's the one who refuses to accept the situation we're in, and in Russia, if she wants to be stupid and die, let her,"

"Goddammit, Nessa, she's OUR friend, and WE'RE being hunted, not JUST US but HER too. We have to do what we can to stick together; otherwise, they will use our confusion against us," I replied.

"If I were them, she would be my first target to send a message to us about how serious these guys are, to try and shake us from making it out alive. They thrive off of our fear. We can't give that to them. So please just get your head outta your ass and THINK!" I argued with her.

When I looked back up the road, Fox's frame was almost out of sight.

"If you run into them,"

"Ugh, fine, I will protect her since she's too weak to do it herself," Nessa replied, putting the jug of water down in the trunk of the SUV, grabbed a pocket knife from under the floorboard, and followed behind her.

"Nessa," I said, "Please come back in one piece," I asked as my heart sank to the pit of my stomach. She nodded, "There's another knife in there. Make good use of it,"

"We're gonna make it out of this shit alive, together. I promise," I affirmed with authority, "Okay," she agreed. Then ran after Fox.

I reached under the floorboard, spotted the small flask, grabbed it and the pocket knife beside it, and opened the cap to it. Hallelujah, I thought when I was greeted with the smell of liquor, which smells like rubbing alcohol, but I don't give a fuck anymore.

I took a swig, and as the smooth liquor burned my throat, I shook my head to relax myself a little more into the role I've assigned myself, or the role the group set to me, I don't even fucking know anymore.

Sitting down and tucking myself inside the SUV with the trunk door open, I curled into a ball by tucking my knees to my chest and let my tears fall silently until it was hard to dry swallow the lump in my throat. Not knowing if I can even keep the promise I just made to Nessa about getting out of here alive, with all of us intact. I'm not a fucking leader. I'm just another college student who wanted to graduate as a journalist and write kids' books and shit.

To tell them the world is wonderful cuz I've seen how awful it is, and this was another reminder to me of why it isn't. My tears fell harder until it made a wet spot on my jeans, Goddammit.

I clicked the button on the side of the pocket knife until it showed the blade, like muscle memory I have tucked so far into the depths of my own shadow, the part of me I never wanted to discover, the part of me that never wanted to go back into the hell of that world. Still, now I don't have a choice, I thought, gripping the blade in my hand with conviction.

I will get us out alive. I have to.

Chapter 3: Trauma Bond
Kalina (Fox) Izumi

I can't believe this bitch. Is she fucking crazy??! Talking 'bout some, oh we gotta stay out here and NOT call the cops or at least try to get the fuck outta here, who died and made this bitch the fuckin' leader?! THIS CAN'T be fuckin happening! I thought, wrapping my arms around while trying to ignore this bitter cold. I looked up at the sky, and it wasn't nothing but trees so high it was like I couldn't even see the goddamn sky. I shivered and let my tears fall, God why? What the fuck is happening? I'm too young to die.

This shit is so fuckin cold it was like the air froze my damn tears, but I'm too scared right now, as I kept marching forward towards the main road and ignored the jagged rocks from walking up the dirt path.

"FOX!" I heard crazy bitch Nessa shout, "FUCK YOU! I'M LEAVING!" I argued, marching faster.

"Listen, it's not safe, please come back and stay," Nessa actually pleaded for once, and I stopped, turned, then glared at her.

Is this bitch serious?! I WANNA GO HOME! You know, home in my room and just pretend like this shit is just one terrible fuckin nightmare. I am NOT built for this kinda shit, AT ALL!

"Look, I don't know you, so I think I'll take my chances out there!" I fussed, but when I heard howling in the distance, I froze, and like the air, my blood went frozen like ice. No, no, no, no, please tell me that's not what I think it is, I thought, and when Nessa stomped in front of me looking at some shit in the woods, I can't even see.

"Sis, what is—"

"Shh," She shushed me.

A chill jolted up my spine, and it covered my body in goosebumps until more tears stung my cheeks, but I silenced my sobs.

Then I heard a growling in the distance, and my heart fell out of my ass when I did, cuz it was loud, like REALLY loud.

"Do. Not. Move." Nessa whispered firmly, "Do. Not. Back. Down." She instructed, "Sis, what the fuck does that even mean?" I barely got out from the dry lump rising in my throat the harder I clung to the back of her Green Coat.

My instincts were telling me to run for my life, scream, shout, something, anything to get me out of this fuckin nightmare.

"Fox. This wolf is an Alpha, so do not, I repeat, do not attack it; otherwise, the rest of its pack will come after us," Nessa warned.

Son of a bitch, are you FUCKING KIDDING ME?!

"I need you to stand your ground, Fox. Otherwise, you will be this damn thing's target."

"Fuck you, Nessa, I'm not standing my ground against a goddamn wolf. Are you INSANE, AND WHY ISN'T THE DAMN THING TARGETING YOU!" I exclaimed in a whisper to not alarm it, but my heart was beating so damn hard, I could hear it in my ears.

"Because I'm not afraid to do what's necessary to fight it off if it ever comes down to me and it, even in hand to hand if necessary,"

"Nessa, I can't take much more of this shit; I'm gonna have a fuckin heart attack. I wanna go home," I kept reminding, I don't belong here. I never did no shit like this, ever, in my entire life.

"Let me explain one thing if you get bit; it's over for you. So you have two choices, fight, or die." She said with authority in her voice.

"Fuck you, you can't ask me to make that choice," I trembled, clutching onto her coat for dear life.

"Then you will die,"

"I CAN'T die," I cried.

"I promised Tessa I would get you out of here and bring you back with us. Whether you come back in one piece or not is not up to me."

"Then fuck it! I'll die then! I would rather die than to live another minute of this fuckin nightmare!" I finally admitted, "then so be it," she replied so nonchalantly.

When she stepped aside and walked in reverse, not turning her back to the damn thing, I finally saw it. It was a big ass grey wolf baring its teeth at me in a snarl, and I shuddered, and my tears wouldn't stop flowing.

"Nice doggy," I said, and when I turned around, Nessa was gone.

God, why is this happening to me?!

At that moment, it was like everything went silent, the birds stopped making noises, the air grew thick, and everything went still when I turned around and saw the wolf leap for me. It was like in slow motion as it was mid-leap, I'm going to die. This wolf is going to kill me, and I'm going to fuckin die.

Then like a flash, I remembered my little sister Kana. She was staring at me in the casket, crying. She's only ten years old.

No, I can't die. It can't end here. I have to live for her. I promised to protect her, didn't I? I promised to be there with her at her wedding, to see her kids grow up, FUCK THIS!

As the wolf lurched, I spread my legs shoulder-width apart to hold my stance firm and raised my arm to guard my throat since I didn't have enough time to run. The wolf sunk its teeth in my arm, and the blood gushed from my forearm, then splattered against my face as I hollered from the searing pain and the way its teeth crunched into my bones.

"FUCK YOU!" I shrieked using all the strength I could muster to ball my other hand in a fist and pounded it in the center of its forehead, one, two, three, four, "GET THE FUCK OFF OF ME!" I shouted.

And I was in so much pain, I couldn't feel shit, so I closed my eyes and kept pounding its head until it would release its grip on my arm.

Since my eyes were closed, I heard slicing, carving, and the wolf yelping in pain until it eventually went slump and released its grip on my arm. What the fuck just happened?

Then when I opened my eyes, I saw Nessa standing beside me with her hands and face covered in hot blood splatters, and I was in too much pain to feel anything other than my blood dripping down to my fingertips into the dirt.

I finally looked back at the wolf as it laid there, lifeless. Dead.

No, this can't—this is happening? This is really fuckin happening. I'm not dreaming cuz this pain from my arm is telling me I'm not.

Cuts and bruises from when she slammed on the breaks earlier tell me it's not a dream.

Nessa said some shit to me, but I can't hear her, I can't hear anything, the burning, throbbing pain in my arm is too much for me to handle, and the air is getting really thin. I'm lightheaded. It's hard to move. I can't move.

Everything slowly faded, and when I felt my body hit the ground with a thud, I glared at the trees and the dark sky, as it all encased itself around me, like a goddamn coffin. There, you happy? I stood my ground like you said. And I still fuckin died.

Tessa (Red) Parker

"**F**ox is injured! MOVE!" Nessa shouted.

I perked my head up, gripped my knife, and when I caught sight of Nessa carrying Fox over her shoulder, I scooted back into the SUV as Nessa plopped her into the back with me with a thunk in front of me, and I noticed the blood that covered her hoodie by her arm. Then the bite marks. My heart plummeted to the pits.

"What the fuck happened?!" I asked, trying to calm my erratic shivers, "She was bit by a wolf. We have to stop the bleeding," Nessa explained.

"GODDAMMIT!" I pounded my other fist in the cabin of the car, "I told her ass not to wander off! Please tell me you got some first aid shit in here?!" I demanded.

"I do, but for now, I'll grab the towel, you wrap it around, and I'll look for the first aid kit," She said, springing into action.

"Got it," I affirmed as she reached into a pocket near me and tossed the white-colored towel, "Do not remove the hoodie yet," she told me.

We both hurried to patch her up, and thankfully she was passed out for most of it. Otherwise, if she were awake, she would be screaming and hollering the entire time. Except for when we had to cauterize the wound to close it, then she was kicking, screaming, and crying. But I did all I could to hold her still while Nessa did what she could to close it, "I'm sorry,"

"I fuckin hate all of you!" She kept saying over and over again.

All I really wanted to do was hug her, but I am too fuckin exhausted cuz my stomach is gnawing at me, and it's like getting colder the longer this shit goes on. Not good.

She ended up passing out again when we were done, and we bandaged her up, laid her down in the trunk with a pillow and a blanket while me and Nessa sat in front of the fire we made. Thankfully I had a lighter cuz I never leave the house without one for this exact reason, fire is everything. I can't tell you how fast me and Nessa moved just to treat Izumi for the simple fact that we knew between us.

But we needed food like yesterday.

Nessa decided to go hunting with just her knife, and I decided to stand guard of Izumi if those psychos wanted to try any shit with us. Stone can handle shit on her own, that's one thing I can rely on, but if she's not back by a specific time, shit, speaking of, what the hell is the time?! I thought, grabbing my cell phone in my pocket: "10:08pm"

SHIT!

If she's not back in twenty minutes, I'll have to assume she's dead or someone went to snatch her. Between Nessa and me, we know the rules in this kinda situation; if she's not back by a particular time, there won't be a search team cuz right now, Izumi is dead weight right now and is a liability to the team.

I abandoned this line of thinking a long time ago, only to realize this is what's needed for us to survive. And it's weird to say, but I kinda get the feeling Stone would be okay with that, as she considers it a disgrace if she died hunting. I did learn a little bit about her culture when it comes to this kinda shit.

Ten minutes, passed and the owls hooted, other animals I can't identify grumbled, and more animals cawed as the wind bit at my cheeks from the frigid air. Goddammit.

My eyelids were getting heavy, and my stomach kept gnawing and growling at me in protest. No, don't go to sleep yet.

Then when I heard a twig snap, my stomach clenched, and I jumped to my feet in front of the fire where I listened to the sound, then took my stance, and held my knife up, "Whose there?! Identify yourself!" I shouted.

"Nessa! I come bearing gifts!" She laughed when she stepped out of the shadows holding a few rabbits by the feet at the bottom.

It was like by her admission, my body slowly waned until I plopped hard on the ground, and when I did, it shot a sharp pain up my spine from the impact, "OW MOTHER FUCKER!" I griped.

"You may wanna be quiet. They're still out there," She giggled, walking closer to the campfire.

"Well fuck you, Nessa, my ass hurts, I'm tired, cold, and fucking hungry," I reminded with a groan in frustration.

I turned around to where the SUV was parked to make sure Izumi was still sleeping peacefully and that no one snuck around to kidnap her or some weird shit since we were a couple of feet away from her. I think it's safe to say they're watching us to see how we survive the night and then will probably chase us in the morning.

This is not some fuckin Hunger Games shit! What the fuck is wrong with these kids?!

"Nessa, I can skin one," I told her, and she eyed me confused, "Do you know how?"

"Yeah, I do," I reluctantly admitted reaching my hand out to her so I could do my part, then she smiled, "I won't ask," she got the hint.

Please don't. That's a part of my life I never wanted to be reminded of cuz I'm running from it. But I don't have a choice anymore.

I promised to make it out of here alive, with everyone.

As our dinner was cooking over the open fire, me and Nessa said nothing for a little while, letting the sounds of the night woods encase us. Crickets were chirping—the animals were groaning and grumbling. Birds cawing and hooting, obnoxiously loud, as if to remind me the entire reality of the situation. We're stuck out here and are on the run for our fucking lives. How the hell did this happen?

Since Nessa was sitting next to me, she pulled me into a side hug, "Are you okay?" She asked me.

"Yeah, why?" I asked, confused.

"You're crying," she replied while rubbing my arm up and down to comfort me, and the warmth of her made it hard for the emotions not to bubble inside of me, "Yeah, I'm fine, Stone," I said, swallowing the rest of my tears.

"It'll be okay like you said; we'll make it out alive," Nessa mentioned, and it was like we finished each other's sentences.

"Fucked up and wounded,"

"But alive," She finished for me as if somehow giving me the strength I needed to make it through this bullshit nightmare.

"We'll take shifts," I said, "Agreed. I'll go first, it'll be hard to keep time once our phones die since there's no electricity out here, but I'll wake you up when I get sleepy," Nessa commented.

"Sounds good," I agreed.

When the food finished, we decided to wake up Izumi and give her food first since she was the most traumatized. Despite her daze, she smelled it and devoured it, not paying attention to what it was; thankfully, Nessa brought enough back for us to all eat. I drank some water, laid next to Izumi, and wrapped a towel around my arms since Izumi was using the blanket, then pulled up my hood and decided to sleep as best as I could.

I'm gonna need my strength for tomorrow.

Chapter 4: Kill or Be Killed
Tessa (Red) Parker

I jolted from my sleep when I felt a gentle nudge only to realize it was Nessa waking me up from my slumber, son of a bitch. I'm still on edge from all this bullshit.

"I sleep now. Here," Nessa said, giving me her knife, and we traded places where I sat in the SUV trunk and tried to ignore the cold wind that blew inside the cabin.

I rested my forearm on my knee, gripping the knife in my hand while Fox's snoring made me smile at her ability to get comfortable finally. I looked to the sky through the tinted window of her door and noticed the sky was getting lighter as the air filled with the sound of a few birds chirping, signaling that it was almost time for us to get up and figure out our next move.

Cuz right here, we're sitting ducks just waiting to be killed, even though all the resources are here, so maybe we should figure out a way to fix the car, or should one of us split up and look for help, which I'm probably better off doing that since Nessa don't got a problem doing what's necessary to defend the campsite.

But what if they split up and pursued us? I shut my eyes for a second and focused my thoughts.

What would I do if I were them? Remember how many were there? One beside my driver's side, a black kid, two on both sides of the backseat windows, so that makes three, and two more by the trunk, so it's a total of five of them. Son of a bitch, that's way too many to take on right now. We damn sure don't have the manpower for that; it's better to have three against one versus splitting up.

Assuming I'm the hunters and if I had a home base, maybe a cabin in the woods, and all the weapons, including a map of these woods, and I was hunting me, what would I do next? Something inside told me they'd done this shit before, I could tell from the way he held his gun to me; same as the other ones behind me even if I couldn't see them entirely.

We're sitting ducks, so knowing me, if I were them, I would try to scare me by firing a warning shot to get all of us to run further into the woods, lost, dazed, and confused. Then divide and conquer. But from where? Where would they shoot from?

And I shot my eyes open as it hit me, from high above the ground in the trees: five hunters, three prey. Two would be in the tree's and the other three would hunt us from the ground.

I huffed and gritted my teeth. Please, God, let me be right because I know that's what I would do if I were the hunter.

It's hard to make this decision, but one of us has to play decoy, and the other two need to get their ass in the tree's and fire, and I know the perfect bait, but the fucked up thing is, she would never go for it, cuz she's not strong enough.

Nessa and me are the stronger players right now, and it would make sense for us to ambush them as they're chasing her through the woods. But we gotta find they asses first, and I know me, if I was confident like how he sounded, that's exactly what I would do.

So how do we take them out? I thought while glaring at the tree's trying to think of a way for us to climb up there so we could nail them, but it would take a few days for us to explore the goddamn woods, and they're the ones that have the fuckin advantage. So there's really no way for us to tell where they would strike first.

But if we run further into the woods, we could use our "pretend" disarray to make certain points in it. Cuz three against three is pretty good odds, but tricky. And Nessa said she's outta bullets, so we gotta do this shit the old-fashioned way, up close and personal, and Fox is injured.

Son of a bitch, our odds are slim. Real fuckin slim.

"Hey," I heard Fox mumble breaking me from my thoughts, "Hey sis, you doing okay?" I asked, turning my attention to her for a second.

"Listen, I wanna apologize to you and Nessa," She said genuinely.

I blinked, shocked at her sincere expression, but seriously fuckin grateful that she might be able to help us all get outta here.

"It's cool, don't worry about it. I'm just glad you're alive," I reminded.

Her lip quivered, but she bit down on it to stop the tears from coming, "sorry for being such a bitch, I, I just can't believe this is really happening, ya know? Like how the hell did we go from college students to this shit?" She shivered.

"Izumi," I stated, "Yeah?"

"Please understand something when I tell you, you're right, I'm not a normal person. So everything you said yesterday was true about Nessa and me. I can't speak too much on my background and why, but I'm sorry I lied to you. I really hope you can forgive Stone and me," I asked, hoping that she could forgive me.

She sighed and looked down at her injury, "Sis, I'm not mad anymore, it's weird, it's almost like, I don't feel a damn thing anymore, and all I give a shit about is making it home to my family. Back to my little sister. So for right now, I just wanna say thanks for putting up with me and saving my ass. You've done more for me than people I've known my entire life, real shit. Same as Nessa. The truth is, I'm alive because of both of you. But I'll be damned if ya'll bitches think Imma be like Sakura, and ya'll are Naruto and Sasuke," She affirmed.

I laughed, like really laughed, "I can't stand yo ass," I said.

We both laughed, and it was like I could hear Nessa's sleepy chuckle since I guess she wasn't entirely asleep yet. It was a moment of laughter we all needed to stick together, and make it out of these woods alive.

"We're getting out of this alive, right?" Izumi asked with worry in her voice.

"I dunno sis, but I'm not going down without a fight," I told her.

"You're not scared?"

"No, Fox, I'm scared shitless right now," I admitted, "but I just know the rules of situations like these," I told her.

There was a moment of silence, and the bird chirped louder as the sun kept slowly rising.

"I've made up my mind; I'll do whatever it takes to make it out alive. Besides, for all we know, our parents could've called the cops and are searching for us; I know mine have," Fox said.

I smiled sarcastically, "good, cuz no one is looking for me," I said matter of factly; there's no reason to hide that part about me anymore.

Then when Stone started snoring, Fox I both smiled at each other in understanding.

"You got a plan?" Fox asked more firmly than I thought she would; I guess that bite from the wolf changed her cuz her usual light brown eyes are darker than before.

I looked up at the sky, "I think so, but I'm still going over it; when I got something definite, I gotchu," I commented.

"Let me know how I can help,"

"Bet," I said.

Now that we're unified and on the same page, we damn sure got a higher chance of making out of it alive, especially after hearing what happened to Izumi and how she punched a wolf while it was biting down on her arm, I got no doubts that she's willing to do what it takes for us to get outta here, no matter how gruesome this gets, we have to make it out, all of us.

Tessa (Red) Parker

When Nessa woke up, I came up with a game plan and decided now would be the time to run what I came up with to them, and I know Nessa would agree, cuz judging from her skill base, she's no stranger to combat, and really, neither am I. We all sat huddled together in the trunk with our knives in hand (in case they wanna try some sneaky shit) while we had this meeting, and after I explained my plan to them, Fox looked at me like I had two heads.

"Are you fucking crazy?? That'll never work," She argued.

"Nessa, whaddya think?" I asked her cuz we all need to agree for this shit to work.

She didn't smile at all and shook her head, "I can do it," she agreed.

"Not to be the debbie downer here, but why me?!" Izumi fussed.

I twirled the knife in my hand with skill and glared at her, where she sat across from me, "Because as fucked up as this sounds, you're the injured one, and if our target knows, they gonna gun for ya ass first." I explained.

"Goddammit, this is so fucked up," she gritted her teeth while shaking her head.

"You wanna make it back to your sister, yes?" Nessa asked her where she stood in front of the trunk.

Izumi shot her a firm glare, "anything to make it back," she replied while clutching the knife in her hand.

"Then strong will you must have," Nessa explained.

It was her way of saying, you have to commit to this. Otherwise, we'll all die. The fucked up thing is, Nessa probably accepted from the beginning that if she does die, she would instead go out fighting as she's been trained by her husband, who's in the Russian Military, and those guys are no fucking joke. This is why you never fuck with Russians, ever, cuz they not scared to die.

Izumi took a deep breath and looked at both of us before saying anything.

"Okay, I'm in," she affirmed.

Without warning, Nessa took her knife, and sliced her hand in the center of her palm, and offered her hand to me first, "for honor," she said as the blood dripped down her wrist and met my eyes firmly.

I did the same, grit my teeth, and ignored the searing pain, then shook her hand until our blood mixed, "for honor," I agreed. We knew what this meant; it meant when this shit is over, win or lose, we're sisters both in life and in combat now.

When I saw Izumi's bloody palm offered to Nessa first saying nothing, it shocked me that she even did it without saying anything or crying in pain, but I guess after cauterizing her wound, she wouldn't feel much of shit either.

"For honor, sis," she said, broke from my hand, and shook Izumi's hand with a firm grip, "for honor, my blood sister."

Then broke from her's and offered her hand to me, saying nothing with tears streaming down her cheeks.

We shook hands and agreed, extending the same blood oath because now we're bonded together as sisters for life.

I went to disinfect our wound and bandage it, except for Izumi's cuz her's is part of the plan.

Dear God, I hope this works because when this shit is over, I got some research to do. And maybe my memory is fuzzy from the shock, but I think one of them was wearing our school mascot.

But I can't be too sure cuz it was too damn dark and cold, so I wasn't paying too much attention as I should have. But if they were wearing our school mascot, something tells me it's some real dark, crazy shit going down behind the scenes at our school.

I just hope this one time my intuition is wrong about our pursuers.

Chapter 5: We're All Animals
Kalina (Fox) Izumi

The sky thundered with a single bullet fired, and like I was told to do, I ran down the foggy woods in front with the trees whizzing past me as the cold air pricked the wound in my hand and the leaves and twigs snapped under my boots. *Holy shit, Red was right; they really did fire a shot in the sky just like she said they would; how the fuck did she know?*

Soon after, Red and Nessa followed behind me, and when I turned to look over my shoulder, my stomach sank to the pits; *goddamn, they're fast, which damn sure told me that these people are NOT normal and I'm so out of place here. Mother fucker.*

I stopped and looked down to make sure my blood was leaving a trail in the leaves under me; good, it is. *Hopefully, they'll be stupid enough to chase after it like Red said they would.*

Then I turned to look back again, and they were gone, leaving me out in the open, and my heart fell out of my ass while doing what I could to calm my shaking hand.

My blood went frozen, and my heart thumped loudly in my ears; it was like even though I can't see shit, I can hear them from the way the leaves rustled under our feet, and despite my heart being in my goddamn throat, I did all I could to make sure it was attackers. *Calm down sis; we got this. You're not in this alone. We will make it out of here alive. I have to see my sister again.*

I noticed they stopped, and when the air got real quiet, I gripped my knife and stood still even though I'm shaking like a mother fucker. *Goddammit, I really don't wanna do this.*

When the leaves rustled closer to me, I decided to trust my instincts and dip out, running further into the woods and heard someone chasing me. *Shit, shit, shit,* I thought with my heart racing against my chest and did my best to control my breathing the harder I ran.

30

But my chaser was too damn fast, then I heard another fire of a bullet, and I ducked, noticing the shot had landed in the tree to my right. *Good, they can't see shit like us, bet, which means we can use the fog to our advantage.*

I blinked, and with the wind knocked outta me, my attacker had mounted me, and when I looked at him, I paled. *This guy is in my Philosophy class.*

"**ADAM, WHAT THE FUCK!**" I shouted, but he wasn't listening to me as he kept trying to unbuckle my jeans, "Goddamn, I've wanted you for a long ass time, Fox," he grumbled with his groin pressed in between my legs.

I kept kicking, and when I tried to scream, he forced his hand over my mouth, "Then Imma gut you like the pig you are after I rape ya stupid ass," he laughed. *The look in his eyes is blank, empty, and dark. This can't be fucking happening, it can't be, I took a whole semester with him, and he was so nice to me; what the fuck is happening?!* I let out a muffled scream in the palm of his hand, and in a quick blur, I felt a burning pain in my shoulder as thick blood seeped from it, and I stopped fighting, shivering under his massive frame.

He licked his lips and smiled too wide in his cheeks, "That's a good girl, cuz man filleting the skin off of you is gonna be the best part," he cackled.

I'm gonna die. I'm gonna fucking die. He's serious, and he's not joking anymore, oh my God.

I gritted my teeth and met his eyes with determination as my tears fell from the sides of my eyes, I said anything to get to my sister, and I meant it. *I can't die in a place like this, fuck that.*

"That's the look I wanna see, baby, just like that," he groaned.

Just like Red said, a stupid man would do. It's how I did get my nickname, so like she said to do, I'm gonna use it to my advantage.

God, please forgive me for what I have to do to make it outta here.

("When the man attacks you, take him out with your knife and slit his goddamn throat. Make sure to shut your eyes when you do cuz the blood from his throat will blind you otherwise. Make sure you dig in it, cuz bone is hard to cut through." Red said.

Then Nessa pointed where to cut, "His Adam's apple," was all she said.)

I said nothing and opened my legs for him while gripping the knife in my hand out of his vision since I held onto it for dear life but was too shocked to move.

Then when he sat up to look down at me, I shot up and held the blade to his Adam's apple, "Wait, wait! Stop! Please!" he pleaded.

("He's going to plead for his life, and when he does, you have to tune it out. Otherwise, he will kill you if you hesitate." Red said.

"Hesitate, and you die," Nessa agreed.)

I shivered and swallowed the bile rising to my throat, then closed my eyes and put all the force I could from the only working shoulder and dug the blade in his throat, sawing it left and right.

Since I had my eyes closed the entire time, all I could hear was the blood gurgling from his throat as it seeped onto my hand holding the blade and his attempt to scream, but nothing left his lips, and when he did, I dug it in further, trying to tune out the way the knife sawed his bone and muscle like tough leather.

Then his body thudded to the ground like a sack of potatoes, and I trembled, dropping the blade, I can't open my eyes, *I can't, I won't.*

So when I did and saw his carcass lying there with his throat cut through and his lifeless gaze into the sky, with the blood seeping into the leaves, it was like everything went silent. I'm a murderer now. *Oh my God, I'm a murderer now. He was someone's son, someone's boyfriend, someone's brother. I just—*

And with those thoughts, my stomach churned, and the bile rose to my throat as I turned around and vomited into the ground away from him.

("Don't be alarmed if you throw up for the first time. It happened with me too, because after it happens, it's when hell becomes real and the truth of us, we were never meant to kill each other. But hold onto your reasoning why you did it. Otherwise, you will go insane. I know I did, same as Nessa."

"We only do what is necessary to survive because at the end of the day; we are all animals,")

Are we all animals? I couldn't stop my shivering and crying, and the way his blood stuck to my hands, and the blood from my shoulder dripping into the leaves staining it, the way it sunk into the pores of my skin. *God, please, strike me down now. I can't take this shit.*

Then another shot was fired, and a man's scream filled the air as the birds squawked and flew off. *I'm alive. I'm alive, and he's dead. He was going to rape me, so he got what he deserved, right?*

Get up and move, I thought, trying to force myself up but my entire body felt like lead; *I can't die like this. I can't. I just can't.*

But I can't stop my body from shaking; I can't stop my tears. *What the hell is happening? What is this world coming to? Are we all like this? What the fuck for?* **WHY?!**

Then the adrenaline kicked in, and I was finally able to move as I heard another man scream and shout to the top of his lungs in pain. *Shit, I gotta get outta here cuz the pain in my hand and shoulder is throbbing like a mother fucker.*

So I took my hoodie off to look at my wound and shit; he dug it in deep. *I don't have a choice*; I have to risk infection. *Son of a bitch.*

I took the knife with his blood on it and cut through the sleeve to wrap it around, and tying a wound with one hand is hard as shit, so I used my teeth to tie it, and the taste of my blood made me wanna throw up more, cuz the metal almost tastes like acid to my tongue, and it's fucking disgusting.

I swallowed my bile, grabbed my knife, and tried to get my surroundings again. Then more shots were fired, and with the first bang, I laid on the ground belly side so I wouldn't get hit.

God, I'm gonna need some SERIOUS therapy after this shit is done and to hold my sister in my arms again. Cuz Red is right; I have to hold her to remind me why I wanna live, so please, guys, make it out of this shit alive. Together.

Inessa (Stone/Nessa) Alexeyev

My family is the one who trained me, as we all were at a young age. So doing this, I feel nothing except my will to survive and make it to my husband, and now to protect my new sisters, since all of mine were murdered in front of me, and it's why I am a monster.

So anything to protect my sisters this time, because I was too weak and scared before.

I had already taken two down, and depending on Izumi, if she took down her one, that's three down, and two more to go, which I can take down quickly, and Red can be the backup in case one of us can't take them out.

"YOU WERE NOT SUPPOSED TO MAKE IT OUT ALIVE!" The boy shouted, and I could tell he's sloppy and not used to combat like I am and with that one sentence uttered, I jammed the knife in his temple, and his eyes bulged with the blood seeping from the side, then yanked it out and he fell to the ground.

I decided Red would be okay, so I went to look for Izumi; knowing her, if she did succeed, she's fucked up, and if not, I'll be the one to bring her body home. I've done it once before.

So I bolted to where she was running last, "FOX!" I shouted.

"I'M OVER HERE!" I heard her voice.

I ran to the sound and finally saw her laying down on the ground, "Fox, that you?" I asked.

"Yeah, it's me," She cried. Yup, she's crying. It's her. It wouldn't be Izumi if she weren't crying.

I landed on my knees, and she turned around as I saw the blood covering her hands and a wound in her shoulder with dirt patches everywhere. Damn, I'm out of breath, but I've got to get her back to the SUV. But there's still one more out there.

"I'm fine. Let's get outta here," Fox grumbled.

Her voice changed; she did it. She took her first life.

I lifted her by her other shoulder and handed her my pistol, "for you," and without hesitation, she took it in her working hand.

"Thanks, sis, now let's get this son of a bitch so I can take my black ass home," she affirmed.

As both of us ran back towards the car, I just hoped Red could handle herself as she promised; otherwise, I'd have failed my sisters again.

Tessa (Red) Parker

I ducked, swerved, and maneuvered around him, locked in hand-to-hand combat with the leader. I knew it was him from the way he swiftly moved around, he's the experienced one out of the group, but I left Nessa to go and find Izumi if this plan worked the way I thought it would. But I can't think about that right now.

So I ducked, one cut to his knee, and he fell to his opposite knee, "Goddammit!" he growled.

Then I swiftly jammed the knife in his throat, and he choked as the blood trickled from his mouth, but he smiled, "Bravo, you win the game," he gurgled, and in a few more seconds, his body collapsed to the ground.

I huffed and looked around, one, two, three, four, and I can't see the fifth one.

"RED!" I heard Nessa shout further down and more leaves rustling towards me. I took my stance and held the knife in front, deciding to wait until they approached me closer since I don't know if the fifth one was still alive or not.

Then when Nessa and Fox came into view, I sighed, Thank God, we made it, we fucking made it.

"Is he dead?" I asked Izumi, "yeah, he's dead," she answered.

I looked above, and the sky was getting dark, and since the fog wasn't helping our chance of visibility in this shit, the last thing we need is the animals in this damn forest looking to eat us since we got blood all over the goddamn place. It's cruel, but the best thing would be for any animals to find the dead bodies of our pursuers and eat them to get rid of the evidence.

"Sis, this shit hurts. Can we just cauterize it and get this shit over with," Izumi barked.

"Yeah, let's go," I informed, and we all stormed back to the car, silently hoping they didn't burn it or some shit.

Chapter 6: Mistrust
Tessa (Red) Parker

We ended up spending a few weeks in the woods together, becoming like nomad people, each taking shifts and doing what we could to find a way outta this shit, and when we finally did, we oddly made it back to the campus even though we took the same road back to the city. That's fucking weird? What the fuck?

I glared at the big grey and blue-colored building, and the other students glared at us with an evil eye, and my heart sank to the pits because of the way everything seemed on edge. No girl, stay calm.

"Sis, we need to get help!" She shouted and ran into the building frantically, shoving the double doors open, and we bolted after her.

"What the fuck is she doing!? Doesn't she know that running is only gonna get us fucked up!" I argued with myself. These people are already on edge, and the last thing I need is—-

I stood behind her, and so did Nessa as Fox pleaded to the officer, "Oh my God, officer! We just made it outta of these fucking woods!" She shouted.

"Who the fuck are you?! I've never seen you around these parts!" The black security officer said, yanking out his gun, loaded it, and aimed it at Fox.

She banged her hands on the table in front, "No! Wait, please! It's not us! We didn't do anything!" Fox hollered.

"Fox, shut the fuck up!" I tried to warn.

Bang! And I saw Fox's body wane as her forehead thump against the desk, leaving a bloodstain on his counter, then aimed it at Nessa.

"The Principals daughter Kim warned us of people like you! And cuz I ain't never seen you around here, fuck you!" He hollered.

Bang!

Then I turned to face Nessa's carcass fall to the ground as her blood leaked into the grey-colored tile floor of the school. All the other students maneuvered around the dead bodies, and I paled.

What the fuck is happening? We made it out of all this shit to be treated like THIS!

Why are they so afraid of us? I thought and looked down at my hands and noticed we were covered in blood, with dirty, disheveled clothing. We aren't well dressed like the other students and don't look like normal people.

Oh my God, was my last thought as he pressed the cold end of the barrel to my forehead, "I refuse your kind to walk around this school and infect it. So we'll eliminate you on sight," and when his hand trembled, I saw his eyes.

He was terrified of us.

BANG! Then I fell back, and my eyes met the bright ass lights of the school, and before everything went dark, "DIE DIE DIE!" I heard the other students shout to the top of their lungs and more stabbing sounds beside me.

Tears fell from the sides of my eyes. The students are murdering my sisters. I failed. Then lights out.

Act 2: Division
Chapter 1: Do-Over
Tessa (Red) Parker

I blinked and noticed Nessa, me, and Fox were all standing in front of the same building we just died in; what the actual fuck? Like a bell ringing inside of my head, I grabbed Fox's wrist before she had a chance to run off.

"What are you doing? Help is right there!" She tried to fight with me, "Izumi, stop; we have to stay CALM when we approach them," I warned.

"I just wanna make it back home. The security guard is right there; I see him sitting through the door," Izumi pouted with confusion.

"Calm is the best method," Nessa reaffirmed.

"Goddammit, you guys are always trying to tell me what to do," She frowned, "Because we die if you do that," I snapped.

"Wait, what?" Nessa asked when she turned to face me, confused.

"Guys, I can't explain it, but I just know we die if Fox goes in the way she was going to just now. I saw it." I explained.

"How the hell do you know that?" Izumi trembled as I let go of her wrist, trusting in the fact she was calm.

"Look around you, sis," I told her.

When they did, all the other students were whispering, and I finally noticed each of them had weapons on their hips. What the fuck is really going on?! This has to be some fucking nightmare.

As if sensing the danger we were in, and seeing how different we looked from them, no wonder they would think we were the enemy. We look like a bunch of savages who had been camping in the woods for weeks; I wouldn't trust me either if I was approaching the security officer the way Fox did.

The fucked up thing is, the security officer mentioned something weird before I died, that the Presidents daughter Kim said something about people like us. Is she the one who told those kids in the woods to hunt us down?

She has to be the one behind this shit, and Imma find out if she is or not.

"Guys, we have to stay calm," I warned.

"Why are all of them looking at us like that?" Fox asked, huddling closer to us, and Nessa kept her eyes locked ahead, "Because we are their enemy," Nessa finished,

"But why?" Fox asked, "Because we don't look like them and anyone different from them, and they strike first and ask questions later," I explained. That's how fear works. That's why the security officer shot us all the first time. I can't explain this shit right now. I still don't know how the fuck we are alive in the first place, but I'm so far gone I don't know what's what, and all I give a shit about is making it out of this alive.

Not like the outcome I just saw earlier. Why the hell are we still alive? I thought we all died?

"Okay, I'll talk to them and be chill," Fox said to us both, "We'll stand behind, and Nessa, don't do anything," I informed.

She shot me a stern glare, "I hate weak people," she cursed.

I don't blame her either, cuz at the end of the day, only weak people's minds can be ruled by fear are the ones owned by the system. It's why we got shot in the first place.

Fox did her best to straighten herself up and tried to look like the other students as we all walked behind her to the security officer's desk. When we walked through the double doors, I noticed the way he looked at us skeptically, and I stayed on guard, hoping Izumi would be able to use her charm or some shit to alert for help and not have them shoot us like they did last time.

And why the hell did the other students kill us? This shit makes no goddamn sense, and I'm doing what I can to wrap my head around this fucked up situation as is, and I'm coming up empty.

"Hi officer, I'm so sorry to bother you, but we got into some trouble and need some help. Can you help us?" She asked sweetly.

"I've never seen you around here," he said firmly.

"Right, about that, we are students here. Is it okay if I grab my ID?" Fox asked, now assessing the danger of our situation. Cuz if we tip them off in any way, we'll be shot down like before. This whole thing is so fucking weird; I can't even wrap my head around it. What the hell was that?

He eyed all of us skeptically, "Okay, but if any of you pulls a weapon, I'm shooting you immediately," he warned.

"Right, of course, no problem, officer," Fox agreed. She's the better negotiator out of all of us, cuz I know me, and Nessa would gun his ass down and make a run for it if this shit goes south again.

God, that's so fucking weird to say right now.

She grabbed her wallet from her disheveled hoodie and showed the officer her ID, and since it was daytime, he didn't need to use a flashlight or anything to verify it.

"You guys with her?"

"Yes, officer, I'm sorry, it's just been a lot of shit that happened recently. We got lost and had to camp out in the woods," I lied, deciding to backup Izumi.

"You?" He asked Nessa, "I sorry, sir, I'm not from the states, and I'm here to visit my sisters, you see, so I'm also just as confused and scared honestly," She followed up. Thank God Nessa is good at lying and looking frail when she wants to, but don't get it twisted. I legit saw this bitch kill two on her own in the woods. She is not to be fucked with at all.

"You don't look related," He said, reaching for his taser this time, "Listen, we got lost, our car broke down, and I'm just, I'm so scared, please, help us," Fox covered for us both, and we decided to play the weak woman card.

The last thing I need is for him to shoot or taze us, cuz I get the feeling once he does, those other students would stab us no problem, which is even eerier.

He stopped and released his hand off of his taser, "Alright then, I'll call the police and get you to safety," he promised.

We all sighed, and when Fox turned to face us, she had tears streaming down her cheeks, then winked at us. Goddamn, that girl is good. I have to give her some credit when this shit is over.

As soon as the cops were called, Fox's family was notified of how our car broke down and how we made it out of the woods after getting lost for almost a few weeks, but never mentioned how we were chased by our fucking classmates.

So when I saw her hold her little sister in her arms, she held her for a long time and whispered something in her ear, shivering and crying silently. God,

I know what that feels like, I thought to myself after watching her little arms wrap around her Izumi with earnest.

"Sis, are you okay?" I heard her say, "I'm fine, sis, I'm okay now," and I knew she was saying it more for herself than for her, which I totally get.

"Oh my God! What the hell is going on here?" I heard a woman's voice ask as she bolted through the parking lot, and I knew exactly who it was cuz I saw her photo in the school paper; it was Kimberly Levine who probably came to signify. The hell is she doing here?

Then when she met my eyes from across the way while she was consoling Izumi, I paled at what I saw when her eyes met mine. Why am I the only one seeing shit like this? And what the hell does it all mean?

Kim Levine

I sat on the desk in the chem lab room and twirled the knife in my hand, smiling at her, "Listen, mom, why not just give the school to me? You've needed to retire anyway," I laughed.

I can't stand this bitch, since she keeps stopping me from doing what the fuck I wanna do, and I always get my way.

Her face grimaced, and she snarled at me, wrong move bitch.

"You'll have to kill me before you ever take this school as yours to do what you want with it and its students," She said.

Aww, what a shame.

"You think you can scare me with your tactics and your crazy ass followers? Think again, sweetheart," She warned.

I laughed, "I swear you just don't get it," I said, hopping off the desk and sauntered to her, "I always get what I want," I told her holding the end of the knife to her throat admiring the craftsmanship of the blade I got on my birthday with a dove carved into the blade. It made me smile.

"I should've aborted you," she said with an empty smile.

THIS SCHOOL IS MINE! NOT YOURS! AND SO ARE THE PEOPLE IN IT! ESPECIALLY CUZ ITS A BUNCH OF UGLY ASS BLACK KIDS IN IT!! LET THEM FIGHT EACH OTHER LIKE THE MONKEYS THEY ARE!!!

"You wouldn't dare,"

"Au contraire mother, for the money and ownership of this school," I smiled, then dug the knife in her throat as she choked. The blood trickled from her wound onto my hand and looked her in the eyes as she looked at me with shock, "I would," was the last thing I said to her, rotating the blade until her bone crunched from turning the knife, then dragged it down, slicing her chest open until she bled out reaching for the air to stop me.

I stepped back, and she fell to the ground face forward, "Janitor, clean this shit up," I said, wiping the knife under my blouse and tucked it away in my holster. Then flipped my hair over my shoulder while walking out.

Now, this school is mine. Besides, we can always say she had an accident, and no one would ever know.

Tessa (Red) Parker

Then I noticed she went back to whispering something in Izumi's ear and hugged her; no, get away from her, she's the enemy. She's the one who set us up in the woods. I can't say how or why I knew that, but any bitch that's able to kill her mother for some petty shit like that is NOT a friend.

Nessa stood by my side, eyeing her with suspicion, "what is it?" she asked.

"You don't wanna know what the fuck I just saw," I told her.

"I do, you tell me, now," she ordered.

"Not here,"

Inessa (Nessa/Stone)

"So you're telling me that we all died? How does that make sense?" I asked her confused, there's no such thing as magic or any other weird stuff like that here, not in this world.

"I don't know, Nessa, I can't explain it. Besides, you think if I could, I wouldn't be sitting here having this discussion with you AWAY from Fox?"

"True, but still, it makes me suspicious,"

"Listen, I know that Kim has something to do with this, I can't say how or why I know, but I need you to trust me," she pleaded.

"She's the most respected woman on this campus. How can you be sure?" I asked, needing to know as much information since we had stepped away from the cops for a few minutes to tell me her side while Izumi was getting reacquainted with her family.

My family is all in Moscow, so there's no one to call for me, and my husband is away, so my sisters here are all I have.

"I don't know for sure, but I do know, I can't explain it,"

"Then, for now, I do not entirely trust you regarding her," She was the one who got me set up here at this school and lessened the bullying even if it was only for a little while, I can't see or understand why Red would say such awful things about her like saying she saw Kim murder her mother, that woman was so nice she wouldn't be able to hurt a fly, not like me and Tessa. She's not dangerous at all and is a civilian.

"Nessa, please!" She pleaded, and the harder she pleaded, the more I kept an eye on her, not Kim. She's too nice to be like us.

I eyed her sternly, and something about her earnest expression made it hard for me to ignore her completely, and deep down, something told me she was telling the truth. However, I still refuse to believe it, at least right now, until I get some hard proof and not some crazy vision she claimed to have. Red has always been the off-the-wall one and always brought trouble to her wherever she went, even if she means well.

She already claimed that we died once already and that we all came back to life, but I have no memory of us dying, as I'm sure I would remember us dying. It's the other reason I'm having a hard time believing her at the moment.

But I will believe her for now since I am alive because of her plan. But only for now.

Chapter 2: You're The Enemy
Tessa (Red) Parker

O nce things finally calmed down, I tried to warn Izumi about Kim and how I don't trust her based on what I saw.

"Come on; you're really saying we ALL died and that Kim is behind what happened in the woods? That's really far-fetched, even for you," Fox said, sipping her soda where we all sat together in the cafeteria like it was before the shit with the woods. There's so much strange shit going on here; I have no idea where to start; it's like, that shit really felt like a bad dream, but I KNOW it's not. From the time we survived out in the woods, from the time we made it out alive.

What's even weirder is literally no one is talking about the death of those five kids we killed in the woods, like am I the only one who has all these fucking questions? Am I the only one who cares? Why is it all of a sudden we get to civilization, and now everyone wants to pretend like nothing awful happened? Are people really this weak-minded?

"Do any of you remember?" I asked earnestly.

Fox looked at me with a forlorn expression, "yes, sis, I DO, and I honestly just wanna forget all about it if that's fine with you," she explained.

"Nessa?" I turned.

"She was nice to me when I first got here; I don't see what you see," She said.

It was like I had been sucker-punched by my friends. Why don't they believe me? We took a blood oath, so why don't they believe me? Is this what happens as soon as we get back to being 'civilized' again? We just sweep it under the rug?

"I don't believe this shit, after all the shit we went through?" I said as if I had been stabbed in the back, and when it went silent between us, I decided to get up from the cafeteria table and storm off.

Fuck them; I don't need them, I'll find the truth on my own, I've been alone this long, and since I've died already, I REALLY don't give a fuck about dying anymore.

"Excuse me! Is the Presidents daughter Kimberly around?" I asked the janitor, and when he turned to face me where he stood in the hallway of the bustling students dumping the trash, I paled; it was the same janitor I saw in my vision. My heartbeat against my chest, and I tried to steady my breathing.

He smiled a warm smile, "Oh sure, she's in the office, but I think she's in the middle of an appointment," He explained and returned to his job.

I'm losing my shit. I have to be. I know I am cuz I got no way of explaining what the fuck happened in the woods when I heard the dude Nessa kill say, "we weren't supposed to win," and then the security officer shooting us and saying Kim warned him about us.

Something strange is going on, and it could just be my paranoia, but some shit is going down, and I can't relax until I find out. To hell with classes right now cuz I was failing that shit anyways.

I looked down the hallway that read the principal's office; I braced myself and shook the tension from my hands; it's time to figure some shit out on my own since I can't trust my so-called 'friends' right now. They need concrete evidence to believe me.

I'll prove to everyone; I'm NOT crazy.

When I saw another student open the oak door and walk through towards the crowd of students shuffling up the steps, I decided to knock on the door, "Excuse me?" I asked.

When I peeked inside, I noticed she was shuffling papers, and the office was big as shit with a huge bookshelf and all wood from the shelves to the floor, to the desk, and the expensive kind. Yeah, she would be sitting pretty after murdering her fucking mother, ugly bitch. I hate people like her, who would murder for money and power, cuz she's no different than me, and it makes me sick to know the truth of it.

"Oh yes, come in!" She said nice and chipper, and when I did, I shut the door behind me, "I'm so sorry to bother you, but I needed some advice," I lied, deciding to use the incident in the woods as bait.

Then she finally met my glare where she sat in the expensive leather chair and smiled warmly, exposing her perfect white teeth, "Sure, please have a seat; you look familiar? Where have I seen you before?" Kim said.

The warmth of her voice was unnerving, and I needed to calm my breathing; otherwise, my instincts were telling me to attack her, and I can't when I don't have a reason to, not yet.

"I think I saw you the day me and my friends made it out of the woods from when our car broke down, you remember?" I asked, walking towards the leather seat in front of me, slung my backpack down on the floor, and sat down.

Give me something, I thought and finally noticed how she blinked with shock and plastered a smile on her lips. It made my stomach churn at the sight. She knows something. Is she the ring leader?

"Oh right, I remember. I'm so glad you all were able to make it out alive. Is that what you wanna talk about?" She asked in a chipper tone.

"I never mentioned anything about alive," I told her, and the air got real thick with tension as she said nothing.

"Oh well, I figured if your car broke down and you were staying out in the cold for weeks, you probably would have died," she said too calmly as her blue eyes narrowed, but her lips were curved in a smile.

"Right, we did stay out there for weeks, and it was really bad,"

"Well, I'm here for you, sweetie, since my next appointment isn't here until 5:30 pm. So I'm all yours to talk to until then,"

Good, Imma nail this bitch right now.

"Oh, thank you, sorry to take up your time," I apologized, deciding to relax in the chair since it was super comfortable and I damn sure could use a nap; I haven't been sleeping much since we made it out of the woods alive.

"It's alright; I can't imagine how terrifying that must have been for all of you," I bet you can bitch.

"It really was," I admitted, deciding to play weak to corner her where I want her, this is psychological chess, and I plan to win.

"Tell me about it," She said, leaning towards me and placed her skinny elbows on the desk intently studying me like a hunter would its prey, and I know what that feels like, uh-huh, another indicator. She's not a civilian like I thought.

Why the hell would she want to get rid of us anyways if that was the case? But in my vision, she did mention something about Monkeys cuz most of us are predominately black with some white kids in this school, but that's still not reason enough, not to me anyway, unless she's a fucking psycho like those guys we killed out in the woods.

"Well, I gotta tell ya, I damn sure can't sleep much anymore these days; it's just so hard to get back to reality, ya know?"

"I can't imagine; I'm so sorry," she pitied me.

"Well, needless to say, my memory is shot to all hell, and I'm just kinda in a daze," I said.

"Well, here, I'll give you the number to the school shrink; I'm sure she can help you out," She said, pulling out the drawer beside her, and I noticed the same knife she cut her mom with bingo. Even though it's clean, it confirms my vision cuz of the carving of the Dove on the backside.

"Oh, this? It's a birthday gift from my dad anytime we went hunting," she said, pulling the knife out and showed it to me; sneaky bitch, she knew I was watching. She's more dangerous than she lets off, and now I know to watch her from now on, and I don't trust her as far as I can throw her.

"Isn't the carving so pretty?" She giggled, "Dope blade, actually," I answered honestly while trying to erase the sight of it covered with her mom's blood.

"I know, right? Anywhoo, here's the number," She said, putting the knife away and handed me the card. I took it and gathered my stuff, "I gotta get to my next class, but thank you for your help," I said warmly.

"Of course! I'm always happy to help!" She replied.

I grabbed my stuff off the floor, and when I walked to the door, I stopped, debating if I should say what I should say, but fuck it, I've died once already; what's another time?

"Also, my condolences for the death of your mom; I can't imagine how hard that's been on you," and it got real quiet. It was so quiet you could hear a needle pin drop to the hardwood floor and the tension was super thick you could cut a knife with it at the same damn time.

"Thanks, girl, I appreciate that," she replied.

"No worries, anywhoo, thanks for the chat; I'll definitely be in touch with the shrink soon," I said.

I looked over my shoulder for a quick second, and it was like her expression had melted altogether until she looked like something so grotesque and evil it shot a jolt down my spine and froze my blood at the same time. Then she smiled, "Of course! It's my job to make sure all the students here are safe, healthy, and happy," she explained.

"Either way, I'm grateful," I said, "Have a good day!" And with that, I gripped my bag and walked out the front door.

I have to warn them about her. She's the one who arranged everything; I made a promise to them that I wouldn't let anything happen, even if I am pissed off at the whole thing and them not believing me; I still love them; I still care for them. They're the only family I have now, so I will do what I can to warn them about her and stay on guard.

We aren't out of the woods yet like we think we are, and that's the scary part, we thought the woods were bad, but this shit in real 'civilized' real life is even more dangerous than that, cuz you have no idea who's on your side and who isn't.

Chapter 3: Our Beliefs
Tessa (Red) Parker

I didn't speak to my girls for a few weeks, and they tried texting and calling me, but I wasn't answering. It was hard for me to believe that they DIDN'T believe me, after all the shit I did for them to get them out of the damn woods. This whole thing reeks of Kim being behind the attack of us in the woods cuz she seemed way too comfortable, especially after that vision I had. On top of that, I still can't make sense of how the hell we're all alive after seeing my friends murdered in front of me when we made it out of the woods.

Or maybe I'm just someone with a fucked up imagination, and it all never happened. It's like no one around us remembered the way we came back, even though I coulda swore I saw all the other students carrying knives and shit.

Not gonna lie; there's a huge part of me hoping I made this shit up and the nightmare of us surviving in the woods didn't happen. I really hope the vision I saw about the Presidents daughter wasn't real, but I know myself well enough. I have a gift. A gift no one can understand, and I got one of two options; embrace being the crazy one, or run from it and pretend to be normal. But what the fuck is normal anyways? I thought, taking another long swig of the bottle of honey jack I had clutched in my hand and savored the burn in my throat when I drank it.

I looked at the school where I sat on a tree limb and inhaled the warm dewy air since it's getting to be springtime which means a field trip is coming soon. It's stupid shit, really, but if my instincts are correct, something tells me this is gonna get really gritty if it's gonna be where I think it is, cuz I've been having nightmare after nightmare since the incident, and I can't share those with anyone. It's why I said I might as well accept being fucking insane.

Dear God, please let me be wrong about my intuition cuz I don't want anyone else in danger anymore.

Inessa (Stone/Nessa)

I hadn't heard from Tessa in a few weeks, and now I'm worried about her. She may have gone off the deep end, but I understand, after what we went through, it took me some weeks to finish my emotional processing of what happened. But those kinds of things like having abilities and powers are not real, so why would she be so insistent. Perhaps she has a mental illness I do not know of?

"Hey, Nessa?" Fox called out where we sat in the library studying for our exams, "Yeah?" I asked.

"I'm worried about Red," she whispered with a forlorn expression.

I looked down at the anatomy textbook in front of me, "I know Fox, me too," I admitted.

"The shit that happened," she paused, "it was real, wasn't it?" she asked me.

"Yes, it was Fox. I'm sorry," I told her since we hadn't talked about it and chose to forget it, which is usually the best thing. Fox and I decided against therapy per Red's request.

I'm a survivor and relate to Tessa, but not when she's erratic like that. Still, I noticed something odd, something I never confessed to her since the incident, Kim had been getting close to Fox and me and asking questions, the type of questions no one else would know or even think of, and it had me alarmed. So now, I have my doubts about everything right now. I know what a predator feels like, and it's still, even now, hard for me to believe that Kim would be capable of something so gruesome like Red or me.

"I hate this shit, I hate not being able to sleep, I hate hearing shit in the middle of the day, and I know Red if she's the one whose been having all this bullshit prophetic stuff happening to her, something tells me she's going through it the worst," Fox murmured.

"Something tells me something is off too; I just don't know what," I said, gazing at her sternly.

"Nessa, I know what Red said is fucking crazy; hell, I don't believe it either, but I'd be lying if I didn't at least admit when she told me not to do something or how to handle something, she was right. Even if she couldn't justify it, hell how would you justify what happened and how she just knew how they would attack us in the woods? There's really no fucking way she could've known, and she did. I'm alive because of you both," she reminded.

She's right.

What harm would it do in listening to her, even if it does sound insane, but it would take an insane person to get us all out alive when we weren't supposed to at all. I'd be a fool not to admit that much, at least.

"Hey, guys!" I heard Kim call out to us, "don't say anything," I warned Fox as if we were back in the woods, and she picked up the cue. It reminded me why we work well as a team now.

She said nothing and returned to her notes as I turned to face the sound of heels clicking against the floor, smiling, "Hi Kim," I said.

"Hey, girl! I figured I would join you guys for a study sesh, cool? Great!" She said, not waiting for either of us to answer, and plopped her designer bag on the table in front of Fox and me. Rude.

She sat in the chair next to me, where we all sat around the rounded table inside the library with other students shuffling around and light talking nearby.

I turned to face her, and she fluffed her hair before turning to face me with a wide grin, "Sooo, how's it going?"

And since I couldn't see Fox over her big designer bag, I waited for Fox to cover for me, "Oh, we're good, I'm studying for my chemistry test, and Nessa is studying for practical," Fox chimed.

As the weeks passed, although we didn't talk about the incident, our trust grew for each other where we had more nonverbal cues than not because I taught her not to have them is to die.

Since Fox promised her little sister to make it back to her no matter what, I knew she took my words seriously regarding stuff like this and trusted my leadership. Especially since Red isn't here with us right now, I needed to know if what she was saying was right all this time.

I can't imagine someone who does so much for the school could be as evil as Red thinks she is, but she has been nosier than I care to admit, and now thinking back on it, why is she? I mean, why us?

"No fucking thank you," she laughed.

Kim pulled out her textbooks, slammed them on the table, and set her bag down on the floor, then turned to face us, "I gotta be honest, history is way cooler than the sciences only cuz I can always imagine hot guys killing each other for me as the Queen or the Princess, and makes it easier to keep my grades up too," she said with a giggle. Then her phone kept buzzing on the table where she had it sitting beside her books, but she ignored it.

"So, Nessa? How's the hubby? Have you heard anything from him?"

"No, he's off to combat at the moment," I lied.

"Oh damn, that sucks. How are you handling that?" She asked me with sympathy, "Fine. If he dies, it means he wasn't fit to lead," I told her. That is our code of life; it is why we as Russians vowed never to be weak again, and my husband is anything but weak.

"That's heartless, but don't you love him?" She blinked with a confused expression. Fox kept to her notes and was intently listening even though she looked busy.

"I do, but he's capable of handling himself," I told her.

"Man remind me to never fuck with you, ever," she laughed, "Fox, you holding up, okay? I know it's been a few weeks since, well you know,"

"Yeah, it has been, but I'm fine. I'm just happy to be back with my family again," she admitted sincerely.

"Guys, seriously, what happened was traumatic to anyone, and again no pressure, but I wanna remind you that you're safe here. My mom wouldn't have wanted it any other way, especially for the students she loved so much," she said with a sad smile.

Did she murder her mother like Red said she did? And while civilians would never remember something someone said weeks ago, I did.

"So seriously, I'm always here if you need someone whose nonjudgemental, forreals," she reminded.

Fox looked up from her book and smiled at Kim, but I knew she was also just as suspicious of her like I told her to be, "Hey, thanks, Kim, I won't lie and say readjusting hasn't been hard; it has been. But I'm hanging in there honestly,"

"So I was going over the report recently, ya know, for publicity reasons to make sure I got my facts straight. Where did the blood on yall's clothes come from?"

We both shot each other a look as my stomach clenched. Something's off.

"What report?" I asked.

"Oh, you know the police report and the one I had to file with the school since you guys DID show up on school property all covered in dirt and blood. The last thing I need is people slandering the school, saying we had anything to do with it. Seriously, I have a reputation, guys," she mentioned casually.

"So you need our help to maintain the school's image?"

"Well yeah, kinda?" She admitted.

"It was when our car slammed into a tree," I told her blatantly.

Perhaps it was my imagination, but I think her expression went sour before turning into a smile, "Oh gotcha, yeah, that SUV did get wrecked pretty bad," She said.

I returned to my textbook and started returning to the chapter about the bones since I did have a practical coming soon, and I'm just overly paranoid again. I knew Red was making some stuff up.

"Hey, have any of you guys heard anything from Adam Berkly? You know, the tall, lanky kid with dark brown hair? I think he was taking your Philosophy 101 class, Fox, right?"

My stomach clenched, and my blood went cold, and I peered at Fox from my textbook while gritting my teeth as a warning to her not to tell her anything.

"No, I barely know the guy. Why?" Fox said cooly.

I turned to face Kim while she was on her phone texting, "That's so weird cuz he went missing same as some other students, and I'm just hoping nothing happened to them,"

"I hope not, seeing as it would make you look bad, right?" I called out. Otherwise, how would she know the name of one of our attackers?

That wasn't public or made public, but seeing as she keeps a school record of everyone, I couldn't imagine that she wouldn't know. But that IS an odd thing to remember, specifically.

"Ahh, you got me there," she smiled sheepishly, not looking in my direction, "listen, I just wanted to ask in case anyone else had heard anything cuz the authorities can't find him and a few other students, and I honestly just want this whole mess to be over with," she answered with an exaggerated sigh.

"Too much for the Princess to handle?" Fox teased, "Oh fuck you, sis, you have NO IDEA the amount of pressure that's been on me since this whole incident, honestly," She said, fidgeting with the ends of her blonde hair.

I noticed she was unraveling in front of me, much like how you tear off the layers of an onion; when someone is dishonest, their hands begin to shake a bit, fidget with their hair, smile harder than usual, and tap her foot just to name a few. She was doing all of them the longer this conversation continued, which told me now I KNOW she's hiding something.

Then her phone rang, and I quickly saw the caller ID: "Shadow."

"Hey, guys! Gotta run; it's been cool catchin up with you, and again seriously, thank you all for your help!" And she answered the phone, "Hey babe, what's up? How are you? Yes, I'll be right there," She said, grabbing her things and walking out of the library.

"Did you see that?" I asked Fox, "Yeah, I did,"

"Red," Fox paused, "wasn't lying, was she?"

"I don't know Fox. I don't know," I told her honestly, but like Red, my instincts about someone aren't wrong, same as hers.

I guess we aren't out of the woods yet like we thought we were.

Kim Levine

I stormed to my mother's old office, slammed the door shut, and tossed my bag on the floor until the contents of my books fell out, **"WHAT DO YOU MEAN YOU HAVEN'T GOTTEN RID OF THE BODIES!"** I tried not to shout, but it was hard considering what I was just told.

"Listen, fuck you, this shit is a helluva lot harder than it looks, and it's fucking gross. Not to mention **I'M** the only one on the clean-up crew cleaning up the goddamn cabin AND getting rid of **ALL** the evidence before the goddamn field trip we're **ALL** supposed to take to the **SAME** cabin. Some appreciation would be nice right about now!" Shadow mentioned on the other line.

I gripped the phone so hard, it started to leave indents in my palm, "I would do it myself, but I **HAVE** to be here to make sure these fucking monkeys stay in order, am I understood?! It's already bad enough our targets made it out of the woods **AS IS** when they were supposed to be dead, so we could commence the game the way I intended it to be," I reminded. Of course, leave it to the coloreds to fuck shit up.

"Yeah, well, it's your fault for underestimating them, but man did they do a fucking number to these guys, especially Nessa; she's the more dangerous one," Shadow mentioned, and I heard a thud over the line.

I stormed to the massive leather chair and plopped in it, crossing my ankles on the desk, "No shit, Sherlock, she's from **RUSSIA.** Can you believe this bitch told me her husband is in combat and is like, 'if he dies, he wasn't fit to lead' and then on top of that, Fox feeds me some bullshit lie saying she's okay! And it damn sure doesn't help me that they aren't talking to the school shrink about it, so I can get all the intel of WHERE they fucked up and why the students **I SENT ARE DEAD! UGH!"** I fussed, pinching the bridge of my nose from my oncoming headache.

"Damn, that's cold," Shadow commented.

"That's what I said,"

"Yeaaaaah, she is **NOT** to be fucked with," then paused, "What about Tessa?" Shadow asked.

I heard a sizzle over the line, "She's onto me, and I don't trust that bitch as far as I can throw her, we all know Fox is the easiest to manipulate, Nessa is too straightforward, so that's gonna be her downfall, but Tessa or Red is their wild card. She was the one able to read her enemies movements **BEFORE** they struck, and it's how they made it out alive,"

"So she's the leader then," Shadow said, and I heard more shuffling, "Yes, she is, but right now, they don't trust her cuz I haven't seen them hanging out together like I thought they would. And I intend to keep it that way, any means to cut off communication with them, and it makes this next trip easier for me. Now its personal, cuz Red pissed **ME OFF**,"

"What the fuck did they even do, sis?" Shadow asked, "Challenged me by staying alive when I wanted them dead,"

"So simple a reason, why didn't I think of that," Shadow snickered, "You don't think her being distant from her crew is a setup, do you?"

"I doubt it, cuz when she walked in my office last time, she seemed way too intense, which makes me think she's nervous about something she can't confirm, except I don't know what that is, and **THAT** makes me nervous," I told Shadow the truth.

They pissed off the wrong one, like my mother for pissing me off, and it's why she's dead, and the school is mine to do what the fuck I want with it and the students in it. I've never been rejected or told no, ever. Not as the Princess as I've always been my whole life, and anyone who doesn't like it can die.

My dad always called me Helen of Troy for a reason, cuz at the end of the day, she made dudes go to war for her, and I want the same. I want my name in history books, newspapers, magazines, and all of that, even if it takes blood to achieve that goal.

Besides, the rest is because I'm bored and want to have some fun, cuz why not? It's the other reason why the next game will start on the field trip and why I need everything done before we leave for it.

"You think she knows the truth? I heard some of her friends talking saying she's a little off her rocker,"

"Really? Then I could use that to my advantage if that's the case," I grinned widely and ignored the other students buzzing my phone.

"Yeah, I heard her say some crazy shit like she has visions and can manipulate time is what it sounds like, cuz she said some shit about all of them dying when they first made it back to the school. But like I said, she's fucking insane," Shadow told me.

Now, this is information I can use against her, and it made my chest tingle at the thought of winning the game, especially after losing the first time. It'll be the last time.

I intend to expose everyone's weaknesses by using their fear, biases, and prejudices to get the masses to do what I want. It's the oldest tactic in the book taught by my ancestors, and it's why my kind rules the system.

We're meant to be in power and not the filthy roaches with hair that looks like a goddamn brillo pad. History taught me that if nothing else, cuz it's our history, not theirs.

I leaned back in my chair and twirled the ends of my hair, "Well then, it looks like this'll be fun to go against her, seeing as she's the only one comparable this time," I mentioned with a giggle.

Chapter 4: The Field Trip
Tessa (Red) Parker

I walked onto the bus after lugging my shit into the cubby hole of the big ass vehicle, glared down the aisle, and caught sight of Nessa and Fox. Dammit, I don't think I can warn them—and as soon as I thought of it, I saw Kim glaring me down at the back of the bus and noticed it was Kevin, the muscle geek who sat next to her.

The smug look that flashed on her face before she returned to her posse made my stomach clench. Goddammit, she knows. Son of a bitch, no one else knows that our lives are in danger but me.

I ignored her and kept walking down the aisle and ignored the other students gossiping and shot Nessa a look; I was hoping only she would pick up. We're in danger again. Please trust me.

You're the only family I have now.

She gave me a quick head nod, and a weight lifted off of my chest as I sat behind them and said nothing, cuz I saw their heads move to talk to each other like they had exchanged okay's but didn't say anything to me until my phone vibrated.

"U ok?" Fox texted me in a group chat, "yeah, I'm okay, just nervous about this trip, wbu? You guys ok? I know it's been a minute since we last saw each other." I replied.

I scanned my surroundings and noticed how all the students were bouncing off the walls with excitement, except for me. Then I returned to my phone, trying to keep it close to my chest while messaging them.

"Something is off about her," Nessa texted me, "You mean K?" Fox replied in the group chat.

"Listen, guys; we aren't out of the woods yet, so please, just be on your guard for me? Please?" I texted, hoping they would sense my plea.

"Son of a bitch, why can't this shit be over with and I can go back to a normal life? Why does shit like this keep happening to us?" Fox texted.

"Good morning, everyone!" Kim shouted in a sing-songy voice in where she stood at the front of the bus to get everyone's attention.

I wasn't paying attention cuz I was too focused on warning them; when the hell did she walk up to the front? Did I miss that?

She beamed and clasped her hands together, "This trip is gonna be what brings us all together, and I hope you're all just as excited as I am about it. This trip has been paid for exclusively by me, and each of you was chosen for this trip. So I hope you're all ready to turn up and let's have some real fun!" She announced, and all the students jeered.

My stomach clenched. Chosen? Oh God, no, my gut instinct was right. That has to be code for something only I knew, but I hope I'm just paranoid.

My phone chimed again, and it was Nessa and Fox texting each other, "Fox, I know how hard this has been for you, but maybe we should at least consider what Red is saying," and I blinked with shock. Was Nessa defending me? No way.

"I don't give a fuck about any of this; I just wanna be normal and go back to my old life before any of this crap happened to us; I really just want to forget all of it," she texted super quick.

"Hey, ladies!" Kim said to Ness and Fox.

She didn't even look in my direction for a few seconds too long, and something told me she only said hi to them is to prove to me that she's the new leader now. But again, maybe I'm just too paranoid, and I'm really going crazy with my own shit. I'm not so irresponsible I would completely rule that out, though every single ounce of me is telling me otherwise.

"Oh hey Kim, are you excited for this trip? Cuz I know I am for damn sure, I need a break from classes and just life,"

"Oh girl, I get it, being President of this school has its stresses like real shit," She said, and then another student kept pinching her sides as she whacked his hand away.

"Come on, Kim! Come sit with me!" Another guy said while trying to pinch her sides (or love handles, I guess?) But like, where? She doesn't have any.

"Anywhooooo," she laughed, glanced at me, then returned to Fox and Nessa.

Kim tried to sit beside them, but Nessa didn't move when Fox had already scooted over, "Hey guys, I really don't wanna sit in the back, cool if I sit with you?" She finally asked.

"Ness! Move over!" Fox said.

Then the bus started, and with no other choice, Nessa finally scooted over, and Kim sat down. Great, three peas in a pod, and my communication is cut off. What the fuck was that glance over she did at me?

Please let me be wrong.

Nessa

She seemed too insistent, and I noticed she kept peering over to my phone until I shot her a stern look, saying nothing.

"Oh, come on, girl! Spill! Are you able to talk to the hubby orrrr?" She tried to dig, and I do not like when people search.

Especially into my private life when I did not permit you to, yes she was kind to me when I first got here, but it is hard for me not to consider what Red has said about her because if she is telling the truth about her strange ability, I do not entirely believe in, then I'm alive because of her.

"No, I am not," I answered simply.

She frowned and crossed her arms, "Oh come on, girl, you can't be this boring?!" She said, trying to intimidate me.

I do not scare easily, and I have the death of my family to thank for that.

"Yes, I am. Other than my studies, I enjoy reading and collecting knives," I told her, "Oooo, what kinda knives? Like daggers? Pocket knives?" She claimed, and it was like she was drooling, and I did not like it.

I knew not to tell her the truth since she was so desperate to know my hobby too closely for my liking.

"It's been a while since I bought one, and all of my precious ones are stashed away with the rest of my sister's collection in Russia," I lied. I just bought a new pocket knife not too long ago, sharpened it, and brought it with me in the hopes that Red was wrong about Kim.

"No, seriously, she really is this boring, and seriously Nessa, I didn't know you collected knives. That's so not creepy," she joked. But I wasn't sure if she was pretending to be normal while actively listening to what Kim was saying and doing or if she was genuinely fooled by her.

"It's been a long time since I've bought one," I lied.

"Well, you got any pictures in your phone?"

"No, as I do not need to," and now she is irritating me with her persistent questions.

Say I do believe Red for a moment if she's telling the truth about how dangerous Kim is.

The reason she's asking all these questions about my weapons is that she's fishing for information against me, so she knows how to prepare for something that has to do with me, Fox, and Red. And while I would never entirely think that about Kim, her persistence reveals her real intentions.

But if Red is lying because she has a personal vendetta against Kim, then she really is just curious and has good intentions. I'm hoping it's the second option and not the first because a wolf can hide in sheep's clothing.

"Laaaaaaaame," She laughed.

She sat up and then went to mess with the boys in the seat next to us, and I sighed in relief. Red is wrong, and I was getting worked up for nothing.

If she had bad intentions, she wouldn't have gotten up and should have preferred to keep watch over us out of her worry, concern, or obsession with us, though I do not get why and am still hoping it's not anything malicious if she does.

"Nessa, come on, PLEASE just chill the fuck out and tune Red out for just one fucking second, okay? We deserve to live normally for a change; it's already bad enough I can't sleep and hear voices and shit, so just let me play pretend, please?" Fox asked.

I knew what she meant when she said it, but unlike Fox, I was never granted the luxury to think any other way, and it's why I cannot entirely agree with Fox and her whiny need to be a part of a group when she has Red and me even if Tessa is off her rocker right now.

I know she cares for both of us; otherwise, why risk herself to warn us about her? I still think it may be a personal vendetta, but what if Kim did kill her mother for the school? The look on her face was something I couldn't get out of my head the more I thought about it.

But I will play along and observe her just to have someone give Red a chance at the possibility, if nothing else because I do owe her that much, at least.

Tessa (Red) Parker

We were finally able to text, but I knew Fox didn't wanna be bothered with it, so I texted Nessa while Kim was fuckin around with the other guys on the bus, laughing and shit.

"Listen, Nessa, I'm sorry for what I said about Kim, but I need you to understand what I saw in my vision and when I went to go see her in her office, she just gave me a murderous vibe, and I wouldn't trust her. She murdered her mom, fam, and I saw the knife in her drawer she did it with," I finally warned and deleted the text just in case so Kim wouldn't see it if she did decide to snoop over to my side of the fence.

"What did it look like?" Nessa asked me, "pocket knife, hand-carved with initials on it, she said her dad gave it to her as a gift for whenever they went fishing together, but that's the knife I saw her cut her mom down the chest with,"

"But she has no type of muscle; how was she able to cut through muscle tissues and organs? Do you know how crazy you sound?"

"HELLO! This happened like a year ago, but it got swept under the rug, and they called it a suicide; why the fuck would her mother commit suicide, fam?! I may have only come across her in passing, but her smile told me she did care about what she was doing for us, the urban kids,"

"But we are not entirely an urban school and have some rich kids here,"

"NOW we do, not back then when her mother was alive," I texted back, trying not to send argumentative emojis, I hate this feeling of knowing we're all in danger, and I can't explain with actual evidence as to why we are, and it's so fuckin frustrating.

"Red, please tell me you've been taking your meds?"

"YES, I've been taking my damn meds, Nessa; please just watch out for her. That's all I'm asking you to do, and if I'm wrong, I'm wrong, I'll hold that okay," I barely texted back cuz I was shivering with hot rage by her question.

I get it, I take meds for my illness fine, but my illness didn't stop me from getting us out the fucking woods the first time; what makes her think it wouldn't be the case now!?

"Look after Fox too; she'll be the first target again," I mentioned.

"I will, and I know," Nessa replied, ending our texting conversation. I knew it was her way of saying she has her back if she does or says some stupid shit to Kim since we don't entirely understand why she's our enemy. I hate this shit so much.

I locked my phone and did my best to enjoy how the bus drove against the bumps and grooves against the road.

We're going back up to the woods, and right now, I'm fighting that part of myself not to see their faces again. God, please let me be wrong, please.

Kalina (Fox) Izumi

When we made it to our individual cabin's I was staying with Kim, Nessa was staying with Georgia, and Red was staying with Lisa.

Huh, that's weird our group is split up? But whatever, I'm sure I'm just paranoid. No thanks to fuckin Red ruining everything good I have left. Don't get me wrong, she's my girl, but this shit is exhausting; I don't wanna have to be in fight mode all the goddamn time.

Is it selfish to just want to be normal and not have to constantly remember the nightmares? How is that such a bad thing?

I slung my bags over my shoulder with a grin and hopped towards Kim's smiling face after she had told us what the plan is for tonight's bonfire where we get to sing songs, eat junk food, and probably play truth or dare. Ooo, I hope there are drinks involved too; this is gonna be a fuckin blast.

We both walked into the cabin, and it was like one of those luxury cabins you see with all wood, a stone fireplace in the living room, a patio, and a dining room with a glass table in the space. The A/C blew in my face, and I smiled; it was getting sticky since its hot outside, not like how it was when we were in the woods, and it was kinda cold.

She wrapped her arm around my shoulder and beamed, "Well, whaddya think?" She asked, friendly and chipper, while the other male students were bringing in her bags, damn how many bigs did she bring on this trip? So not weird; it's just her being rich and shit, right? It's not like what Red said was true about her anyways, not that I think anyways.

Stop being so fucking paranoid and just chill the fuck out, I thought to myself, grinning in return, "Girl, this shit is lit! Thank you so fucking much!" I squealed.

We squealed together like we had been best friends since elementary school, and the only moments I've had like these are with my little sister. She means everything to me.

So it was weird to have a moment like this with Kim; why is she so excited anyways? I really shouldn't suspect her like this. I'm not like Red. I'm different than her. I'm normal, not crazy like everyone thinks I am.

I haven't been the same since I got back home, and I'm trying to return to being normal.

So maybe this is my chance to redeem myself and not keep thinking I'm the monster that had to kill Adam to survive, but I mean, did I really? I don't know anymore.

"So you want some spiked hot chocolate?" She said.

I looked at her, "Fuck yeah, sis!" She knew whassup.

Oh yeah, this is gonna be a fucking blast.

Tessa (Red) Parker

W hy else would she split us up if she's the one who assigns the rooms? If I were her, I would pick Izumi first as my victim cuz she's still too fucking nice. I think Georgia is gonna try and make a profile for Nessa cuz she's way too removed. Even when she talks, she sounds mean to everyone else, but it's because she's just not a fake person, and it's why I have a feeling Georgia is gonna try and make friends with her or get her drunk like we used to, so she would spill.

And me? I thought while glaring at Lisa's backside, if she's working with Kim to get information out of us, what is it that she wants anyway? Maybe I could get close to her and find out, so I can get my sisters out of this shit. If I can find Kim's motives, figuring the reason for this trip will be a lot easier, and I think it has something to do with the word 'chosen' on the bus.

Please be wrong. I kept silently praying to myself.

"Pretty dope trip so far, right?" Lisa called from the kitchen, where she was making some hot chocolate for herself.

I have serious trust issues, and my PTSD does not help at all.

"It really is. I wonder where Kim got all the money to pay for this shit?" I said, kinda looking around and making a note of my surroundings, where to hide, where the weapons were around the house, and the exits, just in case.

"Girl, haven't you heard? It's cuz of all the trust fund money her mom left her and the profits of this school, stocks and all of that, and don't get me started on her dad Mr. Levine; he's like even more loaded, ugh, she was so blessed," She chimed.

It's cuz they called it a suicide and not a murder. That's why she got all her mom's money. Is that why she killed her?

"Wow, that sucks. Were you around for that?"

"I've known Kim for a little while now, and she was pretty upset about it, especially since she told me they got into a really bad fight a week ago, and

72

it's why she thinks it's her fault until all of her friends like me convinced her otherwise," Lisa admitted.

I heard her footsteps walk towards me, where I sat in the living room on the leather sofa in front of the fireplace—then plopped on the opposite couch beside mine.

That rotten fucking snake, she played the victim to her crime to obtain the trust of all the other students. So she told them a half-truth, meaning she does feel guilty, but not admitting she's the one that did it and felt nothing during the time.

She's extremely dangerous, more dangerous than I thought.

"You don't know much about Kim, do you?" Lisa asked me genuinely, even though I get the sneaking feeling she's baiting me to cling onto any information I can get out of her about Kim.

"I mean, I had an idea, but man, that really sucks. I couldn't imagine losing my mom like that," I lied. The truth is my parents died a long time ago, so I've always been alone.

"I know, right, like that's so hard for anyone, and it's why I think she's so strong for taking her mom's old job to take care of the school like she would have,"

And like a flash, I saw Kim dragging the knife through her mother's chest downward as the blood splattered over her face with a smile until I returned to the present. It made my stomach clench, and I tried to calm my racing heart. She was smiling when she did it, fam, this is not good.

"You okay? I heard about what happened in the woods, about how your car broke down, how did you survive in the woods like that?" Lisa outright asked me, and I knew she was trying to get information out of me, cuz Kim wanted to know more of that too.

But why, though? Unless there's something, I'm missing in this whole picture of why Kim is so obsessed with wanting to know about our time in the woods.

"Yeah, I'm okay; trust me, if it weren't for Nessa having as much shit as she did, there's no way we would've made it out alive," I admitted to her to see her reaction to my comment.

She frowned, but it could be a practiced response and not genuine.

Please, I hate being like this.

"Oh, thank God, cuz girl, I couldn't do it; I'm too damn pretty to be getting my hands dirty like that; what kinda stuff did you eat anyways?"

"Canned food mostly," I said with a shoulder shrug, finally meeting her dark green eyes, "Oh wow, yeah, girl nope, not me," she said, shaking her head.

She took another sip of her hot chocolate, and I returned to my thoughts on the fireplace in front of me while enjoying the warmth of it.

Please, please let me be wrong. Just once, let me be wrong.

Chapter 5: Division
Izumi (Fox)

Getting to know Kim was pretty chill and then hanging out with everyone else was also dope. It just made me feel like I'm finally normal, for once. It had been at least a few days I'd spent with her, and sure I saw her sneak off with her phone in the middle of the night, but I'm sure she was just talking to her boyfriend she didn't want people to know about so I didn't ask.

I just hate knowing somewhere in the back of my brain is the possibility that something might not be correct. Still, I'll keep fighting that thought for as long as I have to, especially if it means I get to be like everyone else and not some fuckin murderer.

I really should talk to someone, but the only reason I'm not doing it through the school is cuz Red told me not to; she did save my ass on more than one occasion, even if I think she's bat shit crazy for it.

When I stepped into the luxury-style bathroom, I looked at myself in the mirror. I smiled, deciding to check out my outfit for the day since she said we were gonna be spending the day in the woods doing some kinda group activity, though she was really vague about it.

I decided to wear jeans, a black cartoon corpse bunny long sleeve shirt, and a scarf with some boots to match. It's warm out, but if we're gonna be out most of the day, more than likely it's gonna get cold, and I prefer to be dressed for nighttime than early morning. I don't mind sweating cuz I love the warm weather and not that cold-ass weather when I was in the woods with Nessa and Red.

My phone buzzed where I had set it down on the cream marble sink, and the text read, "Guys, it starts today; please be ready and don't forget your weapons if you brought any. Sorry for being a worrywart. I love you." Was what the text from Red said to Nessa and me and my heart sank to the pits.

My hands started to shake, and when I looked at myself in the mirror, my hands were covered in blood, and tears had fallen down my cheeks with Adam's ripped open throat staring at me through the mirror. His gurgled scream filled my ears, and I slammed my eyes shut, trying to erase the image.

Then I stared into the sink, turned the water on full blast to try and wash the blood off of my hands, and no matter how many times this shit happens, I can never wash off the blood. I've literally scrubbed my hands raw at one point, and it never goes away, I thought as my vision started to blur when the sink had filled with the rinsed blood from my hands.

"No, please, make it stop," I whispered a cry to myself as my blood went cold, and my ears started to ring a high-pitched ring while my heartbeat filled the drums.

"Hey! You okay, sis?" Kim called.

I snapped from my reverie, and without drying my hands, I snatched my phone and put it in my back pocket so Kim wouldn't see the text from Red.

"Uh yeah, sis, I'm okay," I lied as I tore off a paper towel to dry my hands and toss it in the trash can under the sink.

She was standing all perky in the bathroom doorway with a concerned expression but didn't say anything for a minute.

It's one thing to lie about a boy you're hooking up with and something completely different when you're lying about seeing dead people in the middle of the day.

"Sis, it's okay to talk to someone you know," she said in a gentle tone as she stepped inside and stood next to me, but I avoided eye contact with her, "have you talked with someone about what happened?" Kim asked.

"Yeah, I am; it's just the other stuff they don't tell you how to deal with," I admitted.

I don't know how the hell Nessa and Red can sleep with shit floating in their brains somewhere. They have to be heartless people not to have stuff like this happen to them. Or does it, and they just don't say anything?

Red did say she loves us, and yeah, I haven't spoken to her since the trip, but I do know when she says I love you, it's cuz she thinks whatever is coming, we aren't gonna make it out of alive. She's always been intense that way.

She put her hand on my back and gave it a gentle rub. I welcomed the warmth of it and took a deep breath, "listen, I may not know what happened, but it is my job to make sure everyone is okay for the most part, and to be honest, that's part of the reason I wanted certain people to come with me on this trip cuz we've all been stressed out, and hey, I'm here if you need me okay?" She smiled.

Without thinking, I hugged her, and the scent of cherry blossoms wafted in my nose. It was a smell I welcomed right now cuz anything to remind me that I'm human is something I need.

She held me back, "It's cool, sis, it's over. Whatever happened, you're safe here," she whispered. Nope, not gonna cry. I can't. I'm so over crying.

I'd be lying if I didn't think I regretted listening to Red, even if I know she means well and actually does care, or maybe she just wanted to use me as bait to save her own hide? The hell if I know anymore, otherwise why warn me of anything? Even if it's possible, she's making this all up. Goddammit, I hate not knowing.

Her phone beeped, and she let me go from her embrace, smiling, "Hey listen, is it cool if we all have a bag inspection? I just wanna make sure everyone is safe since we do got bears and shit out here for the group activity coming up in the woods together," She said casually.

But my stomach clenched, and I tried not to glare at her, so I shook my head and disregarded the voice going off in my head, cuz now I'm silently cursing Red for giving me trust issues over the people I've been cool with for more than a week.

But why would she wanna search our bags now and not earlier like when we got here? It would've made more sense then, but now I'm just paranoid like Red, plus it doesn't help that I just got a text from Red that told me that it starts today; what starts today? Don't forget my weapons? I mean, what kinda shit IS this?!

She didn't wait for my answer before calling back, "Okay, cool, thanks, girl! Make sure you're ready cuz we're all gonna head out soon for a group activity in the woods! Buuuut I'm not gonna spoil it, cuz it's a surprise!" She giggled.

My hands started to shake, and cold sweat dripped down my brow while trying to ignore my stomach clenching as my heart raced all at the same time. Please, God, no, please, don't let it be what I think it is. Stop it! It's just Red getting to you chill the fuck out.

"Aiight bet, I won't say anything," I replied with a forced smile on my lips, then I heard her footsteps stomp upstairs where the bags were sitting out of my sight.

I grabbed my phone and checked for more messages from the group chat, "They're doing a search at my cabin now. I have my weapons ready," Nessa texted to us.

"I brought mine. I'm not letting anyone get me a second time," Red texted.

ARE YOU FUCKING KIDDING ME?!

"Guys, please let's just be chill and think about this; what you're talking about is CRAZY!" I texted back fucking up a few words cuz my hands were shaking so bad.

"Don't you think it a coincidence that it's the SAME woods we just got out of not that long ago," Red texted.

My eyes bulged, and my blood went stiff as I tried to dry swallow my spit and stop my hands from trembling.

"I noticed it too; this is the same woods, just a different location, and a new setup," Nessa confirmed.

No, no, it's not. This is different. We drove longer; how does she know it's the same woods. No, God no, please, no, I thought, noticing I was getting tunnel vision, and my ears started to ring.

How much more of this shit do, I have to take?! Why me??

"What makes you think we're their targets?" Nessa asked, and I knew she had a severe militant face right now, and all it did was make me uneasy.

I took a deep breath to calm my hands, shaking like Nessa taught me how to do when my anxiety gets out of control, but right now, it's not working.

"Something tells me we pissed off Queen Bee, and now she's after the three of us, but whose in the shit pit with us, I have no clue," Red texted.

"WHAT IS THIS ANOTHER ONE OF YOUR PSYCHIC PREMONITIONS! FUCK YOU, RED! I CAN'T TAKE MUCH MORE OF THIS SHIT!"

"Pull your head outta your ass, we got a job to do, and that's to make it out of this thing alive, something tells me we're gonna be hunted first," Red snapped in a text, and even though I haven't been around her, I know that look on her face when she said it, even if it's just with words. Son of a bitch.

"Look, Kim killed her mother, but why I don't know, but I do know she suspects me, and if she suspects me, she DAMN sure suspects you two, so please be careful,"

"Where should we meet?" Nessa texted.

Why can't we do shit the normal way? Like talking? Or I don't know, NOT jumping to conclusions like Red ALWAYS does!

"Count me out," I texted, locked my phone, and put it in my back pocket, deciding now would be a good time to trust my instincts even if I didn't like it at all.

Since Kim was upstairs, I decided to do the opposite, and confront her and find out if what Red was saying was true or not; she wouldn't do me like that, right? Not the way Tessa is saying she would.

So I walked up the wooden stairs, and when she held up my pocket knives, I panicked but said nothing, "girl, you know you didn't have to bring these, I know you're scared and all, but jeez, we're safe out here for the most part. Besides," she paused tucking the blades in and I noticed how quickly she did it and it made me sick, "WE should leave it to the guys to protect us," she smirked placing the blades in her back pocket—confiscating my weapons.

"But sis, the guys didn't bring anything, right?"

"Some, not all, why do you ask?" She said, rummaging turning away from me, and kept rummaging through my luggage bag.

"I mean, you're talking about a bunch of dudes from our school protecting the women. That's like a little archaic, don't you think?"

"No, not at all, a man should protect a woman first, and THEN if he dies, I kill the enemy, that's how my dad taught me," she said so casually it made my skin crawl.

She stood up and walked towards me with a pep in her step, "So I'm gonna hold onto these for now and give them back to you after the group activity for tonight, cool?" and not waiting for me to speak up, "thanks girl, you're a real sport," she said walking past.

"Hol' up," I finally said with some base in my voice, and she stopped in the middle of the hallway, "yo?"

"You got any weapons on you?" I asked outright.

She slowly turned around and smiled sweetly, "listen, I know you've been through a lot, and I know you haven't talked to someone, so if you need to stay here in the cabin for tonight until you feel better, that's totally fine with me, though it would suck not to have you there with us," She insisted.

Why am I so indecisive? What the hell is wrong with me?

"LISTEN, I GOTTA TELL you something and promise you won't say anything to anyone?" Kim said where we sat in front of the fire together with spiked hot chocolate in our pajamas.

"Shoot," I said.

"My mom, you know they said she committed suicide, right?" she said with a somber expression, "Yeah, I heard about that, I'm sorry," I replied while sipping my hot chocolate. The warmth of the chocolate-flavored booze permeated over my body until my muscles relaxed.

"So confession, I saw her do it, in front of me and...I just haven't been the same since,"

"You haven't told anyone this at all?" I asked, concerned when my heart sank, and she glared into the mug, "no, no one, not even my dad," she admitted.

"Oh God, Kim, I'm so sorry," I said, "I miss her so much,"

"Did they ever say why she did it?"

"I really think it was the pressure to run the school the way she wanted to, so really, this school killed her, if I'm being honest. Then on top of that, my mom and dad weren't entirely on good terms either, cuz my dad traveled a lot, and my mom just got so caught up with her work and forgot all about us," She explained.

My heart sank, and I stared at her; she looked so helpless and vulnerable. There's no way what Red said is true. No way.

I SHOOK MY HEAD TO get rid of my nagging paranoia, "right, I just think I'll stay here for now and catch up with you guys later," I said.

She frowned, "Aww, no fun, but it's cool. I get it, take care of you first, we'll link up later and listen; this thing may go on for a while, so if you feel better, come join us, okay?" She reassured.

I took a deep breath and smiled warmly, "Yeah, okay, sounds good," I confirmed.

She went down the stairs and out the front door and shut it.

Great, now what? All worked up for nothing.

Tessa (Red) Parker

There was a bonfire in the center of the pit, and since it was dark out, I could only make out the total number of students and tried to remember them by name as best as I could, though my gut was telling me it wouldn't entirely matter.

Kim, Georgia, Lisa, Jasmine, Courtney, Me, Nessa, and Fox.

Neil, Henry, Todd, Nick, Liam, Derek, Oscar, and William.

Kim is the ring leader, Georgia and Lisa are her posse, Jasmine is a wannabe, Courtney is in a league of her own, and then there's me, Nessa, and Fox.

Liam, Oscar, and William are also part of Kim's gang; the rest are just doofus guys for the other girls, though it's hard to tell the skill set of any of them since I didn't go to many of the social parties we had over the week. Something is telling me I should have as Nessa did cuz now she has a better profile than I do, and all I have are my instincts, and whatever the fuck this gift is that I silently curse myself for having it every day.

We all shuffled together and sat around the fire, "So, Mrs. Kim, what are we gonna be doing tonight as a group activity??"

"Oh, you know what it is, William!" Kim enthused while folding her arms across her chest. Good, it's warm outside, and I was smart enough to wear clothing to cover myself in case I needed extra fabric. Where the hell is Fox?

Nessa sat next to me, leaned into my shoulder, and said nothing as we both sat and listened.

"Damn, you guys are so weird and uptight! Chill out, bro! It's a party!" Derek joked in our direction, but I ignored him.

"Why are we here, Kim?" I challenged, and it was weird to hear the group chatter go silent when I spoke, "God girl, I damn sure wouldn't wanna be the guy fucking you cuz you don't know shit about build-up or slow strokin for nothing!" She laughed at me. So did the rest of my classmates.

"Excuse me, I just like my dick straight up, now are you gonna tell me why the fuck we're all out here? Or can I go back to my cabin?"

"No, you can't go back. I haven't seen your ass barely at all this week. Besides, I want us all to play a game, and it's gonna be fun!" She quipped.

My stomach clenched, and when I peered over at Nessa, I think she sensed the shift in the air too and said nothing.

"Damn, Nessa, how the hell did you get married with an intense stare like that?"

"In Russia, strength is what we admire most and not like you American cowards," She called outright.

"Wow, way to throw shade, girl," Lisa laughed.

"So then tell us the story of how you and your husband met? I'm dying to know," Kim insisted as she went to go get the bottles of booze she had in her bag.

"Hell, I'm just still surprised you're married when you don't look like the marrying type at all," Georgia chimed.

"I met him when I was out hunting," she said casually.

I knew what Nessa was doing. She was trying to bait Kim by having one of us say something about ourselves since we've been quiet the entire trip, and thankfully Nessa just gave her a bread crumb to see if Kim would take it by reaction alone since this is psychological warfare right now. Or if she would seem too overly excited, it would be a tell-tale sign of her eyes set on us as her targets. I'm always studying people, and now I know so is Nessa.

Since the fire in the pit illuminated her face well enough for me to see where she sat across from me, I noticed how her eyes flinched with satisfaction before she covered it with an approving grin, "Well, damn you go, girl, that's what I'm talking about!" Kim cheered.

"Daaaaaamn, would you ever think to train me!?" William asked Nessa obnoxiously drooling over her, and she shook her head, "there is nothing to teach,"

"Come on! Show us some moves!" Kim jeered, and so did the other students, "No," was all Nessa replied.

They all sulked and booed her, and that told me right there precisely what Kim was doing; if we were her enemies, she would want Nessa to show off her fighting skills so she could use it against her; I'm on to you, Kim.

I saw what you did to your mother; you're not fooling me bitch, I knew your mother, and sure it was in passing, but she was always kind to me, and she damn sure didn't deserve the death she got. Not by the hands of her daughter.

I remember her smile when she walked down the hallways and how she interacted with the other students, and because I can read people as well as I do, I know she loved her job. Her doors were always open, and the other students I know cared for her, and it's why it was as tragic as it was for all of us; no fucking way was it a suicide. God is gonna have to forgive me one day for all my sins, including all the lives I've taken.

"Aww, girl, you're so fucking laaaame! Fine then, let's get the game started, shall we?" Kim said, silencing the rest of my classmates.

When they all finally settled, I felt the energy shift rapidly into something more sinister, and I gripped the bottom of my seat to brace myself, but for what, I didn't know. I just knew I needed to, and this is the one time I'm genuinely hoping my feeling is wrong.

Even though it never is, and it's why I lost so many people I loved.

"So the name of the game is Cops and Robbers, you know the game, right?" She said excitedly, and I noticed the grin on Lisa and Georgia's face went too far into their cheeks.

"Yeah, what about it?" Liam asked with a grin on his lips, as if he knew where this conversation was going, so I decided now would be a good time to read the room to see who knows what's happening and who doesn't know. The ones who don't know, I have to assume, are the robbers, and the ones that do know are the cops. I think it's a good place to start.

William, Oscar, Liam, Neil & Todd are smiling, and the rest of the boys, Henry, Nick, and Derek, look confused at first but then excited at the thought of us playing this game, probably thinking we're all gonna be drunk playing it, but something tells me we aren't. The other girls Courtney and Jasmine, also look confused but laugh.

So the supposed cops (which I think is code for hunter) are Kim, Lisa, Georgia, Liam, Oscar, Neil, William & Todd.

And the robbers (prey) are me, Nessa, (Fox if she's playing), Courtney, Jasmine, Henry, Nick, and Derek. Shit, I knew I should've gone to more of these fucking outings, but I really didn't wanna be bothered with any of them, and now we're gonna get our ass handed to us.

"Are you guys ready!" Kim said with a giggle.

Everyone else started laughing except Nessa and me, so when she stood up and opened a giant ass bag, and I heard the heavy clanging of the weapons in her duffel bag, my heart plummeted to the pits and fell out of my ass. It doesn't matter how well trained you are. Nothing can ever train that gut-wrenching feeling, especially when it's right.

She handed them off casually to the so-called elected cops, and then Derek was the first to say, "Yo, those aren't real, are they?" He asked suspiciously.

"You all signed a waiver to come here, right?" Kim asked while handing them the heavy guns, and it looked like some surreal shit was happening in front of me. It looked like something I've seen from one of my missions, and it's why I hate this sight every time it happens.

"Wanna find out, cowboy!" William joked, aiming it at Derek and mimicked gunfire without pressing the trigger.

"Yeah, we did sign a waiver, but you put the rules of the game in the small print, didn't you?" I challenged.

After she finally handed all of the 'cops' their weapons and left everyone else like us with nothing, even though I could tell she was smart enough to bring more weapons to cover up if any of these guys fuck up.

"Okay, okay, confession time; you ready?" Kim said in a light tone of voice before sitting down in her chair and folded her leg over the other while the rest of the students sat in quiet apprehension.

The sounds of animals hooting and a wolf howling in the far distance with the chirping crickets, it only readied my thoughts to make it out of this trial alive, no matter what.

"Okay, sooo Red was right, there were details in the teeeeny tiny fine print that says this game is a life or death game and since some of you have to die, well, think of it this way, that people would be happy you're gone," Kim said so casually.

Since her expression finally relaxed under the flickering embers, I was able to make out the disdained smirk on her lips and the blue-black nothingness in her eyes when she looked around the room like we were nothing more than target practice dummies. She didn't give a rat's ass about any of us and was playing nice the entire time like I knew she was.

"Kim, you're joking, right?" Jasmine asked, trying not to shake at the sudden shift of the conversation now that Kim was showing her real face. The rest of the ones holding weapons in their laps started to snicker to themselves, which only built the tension in the air thicker and would make it hard for any normal person able to breathe.

I can tell by the depth of darkness in her eyes, she's killed more than just her mother, and seeing it like that only set me off more than before. I have to try and warn them if I can if nothing else.

"Come on guys, jokes over, this isn't funny anymore, Kim,"

"Yeah, dude, I'm not even drunk enough for this shit yet, fam," Derek laughed nervously.

I felt Nessa's shoulders tense against mine, and I knew she was readying herself for combat, same as me if necessary, though I would hate myself for having to do this shit again. I'm not going back to that life where I was doing this shit for money. I'm not that person anymore. I've changed since then.

"Guys, what she's saying is the ones who don't have guns are all supposed to be the prey, and the ones WITH guns are going to shoot us down,"

"Girl, what the fuck have you been smoking? Kim wouldn't do that to us; I'm sure she's just trying to freak us out with real-looking guns," Courtney defended.

Then everyone chimed after her, "yeah, girl, chill, you're freaking out for no reason," Jasmine agreed.

"I doubt those are real guns," Henry laughed.

"I mean, they do look cool though, but I gotta agree with the rest, what you're talking about is fucking stupid, cuz what would she get outta that?" Derek calmed himself down.

"Damn, girl, don't know how to take a joke. Why is everything so serious for you?" Nick finally finished.

Then when I turned to look at Kim, she had her fingers interlocked together and was peering directly at me with a sinister smile on her lips, "Neil, go ahead and prove that they aren't lethal," Kim said.

Without thinking, I panicked, "GUYS LISTEN TO ME! KIM IS TRYING TO KILL US ALL! Why won't you believe me?!" I finally shouted.

My heart raced and thumped loudly in my ears, wait, why is no one listening to me?! Kim is the enemy, not me! What the fuck!

"Kim wouldn't do that, cuz what would she gain from it?"

"I mean, right though?"

"You do know what happens when you stand against me, right?" Kim teased in that sing-songy voice that's now screeching against my eardrums from how vile it sounded, goddammit, no, she's gonna kill all of us, I don't want to kill anyone else anymore. I left that life a long time ago, and I don't—

I can't go back to that, not like this, not if I can at least TRY to say something.

It was like the room started to cave in, and like they all took some kind of truth serum, it all started spilling out, or is it their thoughts and why they don't trust me? Damn this shit I have. I hate it.

"Look, Kim has been on my side more times than I can count; she's my best friend, so you goddamn right I would do anything for her, especially what she did for me when my dad molested me," Lisa thought loudly inside of my head, which played over what they were actually saying cuz it was too fuckin loud.

Jasmine: "Girl listen, I wanna be like her cuz like she's pretty, popular, and gets all the guys, and fuck if you think I'm gonna be looking like this all the damn time, I don't give a fuck about selling my soul to look and live like her," Jasmine thought as it mixed in with her laughter.

William: "My Grandad told me about nigger bitches like you that would target sweet, beautiful Kim, so if it's her over you, I damn sure pick her. I mean, look at her face; she has the face of an Angel I would gladly die for," William thought.

It was like an onslaught of their thoughts to where tears started to well, and I stumbled back, landing on my backside, but the thoughts wouldn't stop playing in my head.

Derek: "When my parents found out I was bi-sexual, and they locked me inside of a wooden box for two days, Kim was the only one who accepted me, let me cry on her shoulder, and told me there's nothing wrong with me, so fuck you for turning on Kim," Derek thought.

The longer I lay there staring at the sky, the tears fell harder from the sides of my eyes, and I could no longer hear them talking until the trail of my tears trickled into my hairline.

Georgia: "She saved me and became my friend after I was raped by one of your filthy monkeys on this goddamn campus, so fuck you."

Todd: "Dude, no way am I fucking up the chance to hook up with Kim and be seen as the hottest, most popular guy in my life; I'm tired of living broke, paycheck to paycheck and the only way to stop being fucking poor is if I fuck my way to the top. Since no one loved me to begin with."

Neil: "I hate niggers always have cuz me and my family do, so I do too, so I don't need a reason to protect one of my kind,"

Henry: "I'm tired of being alone and ignored; I want someone to see me, my parents don't see me, my mom doesn't see me, all they wanna do is get drunk and work, nothing else. What was the point of them having me? No way am I turning on Kim, not when she's the only one who praised me for my hard work."

Nick: "I'm tired of selling drugs, I'm tired of trying to make it through another day as the man in my house when I ain't got no father. I'm so tired of all these broken homes with single moms raising fatherless kids, so I gotta be the man for my family. Kim was the only one who helped me financially to stop that shit and put food on my family's table, so fuck you. She would never do no shit like that,"

Oscar: "If it weren't for Kim, I wouldn't be where I am now, especially when my parents were sexually abusing me; she took me out of that situation entirely. So no, my side is with Kim. She would never think to hurt any of us. It's why I have the gun, and you don't."

Courtney: "Girl, her name is everything, so forreal me and her family can be on some merger shit, and I never have to go through anything hard in my life ever, cuz the very thought scares the living shit out of me. I could never imagine being poor, so I NEVER wanna be, and I'll do all it takes to have my money to prevent that from happening."

It was like I was suffocating under the weight of their suffering, fear. All of it is fear. They're willing to be killed for the idea of her and not who she really is? No, stop. We aren't different, you and me, so why do we all feel this way?

Can't you see the enemy right there is using our own trauma-related beliefs against us to keep us divided?

"Kim! She's going to kill us, the robbers, and those are REAL guns! Please, you have to listen to me!" I choked.

Nessa ran to my side and looked at me, saying nothing, and I heard all of them laughing at me, "girl, you damn sure got a thing for the dramatics," Courtney teased.

"You won the Oscar for best hype scare performance ever," Henry replied sarcastically.

Then before I knew it, they shoved Nessa out of the way, and when I blinked, there was a gun being held over my head by William, and I noticed his dark blue eyes from behind his blonde tendrils, "These aren't real remember?" He laughed.

The depth of his laugh filled the air until all of them started laughing with him, then boom, an intense, fiery throbbing pain shot through, and the last thing I felt once the bullet went through my head was the thickness of my blood coming out the other end before everything went black.

In the nothingness, I think something became clear to me and why I ended up dead because I always spent more time thinking when I was away from Nessa and Fox since my gift is all I have right now, especially when I was alone from them.

It's the beliefs passed down for generations that have been a curse by the upbringing of our family, and it's caused the mistrust among each other back at the woods between Nessa, Me, and Fox. Now our generational curses are the reason we're divided and not one as the human race, and it's why I'm dead.

Why didn't I just wait to gain their trust and then warn them about Kim? I deserve to die. This is probably for the best since I could never save anyone anyways.

END OF ACT TWO DIVISION

Act 3: Murder

Chapter 1: The Cycle of Death

"**R**ed!" I heard Nessa shaking me, and when I jolted awake, I quickly glared around. Okay, I'm still outside, and everyone still has their guns on them as I reached to touch the back of my head and paled when I felt a little lump where I was shot.

Shit, not again? What the fuck IS that! Why haven't I been able to figure out why I can do that! It's like as soon as I die, or one of my girls die, or we all die, I can come back to life. Or was it a dream? I don't fucking know anymore, but I can't think about that right now.

Then how come Nessa and Fox don't have any kinda wounds like that, and just me?! Wait, is it because I'm the leader. Is this some kina curse of being the leader? I take all the scars, and they get spared?

I blinked myself to attention, "Sorry, I've just been really tired lately," I said, trying not to look in too much disarray.

That's fine. I can handle the weight of a failed leader along with everything else I've ever carried alone. What's another scar added to the list of a million already their scars?

"You were about to say something, but then you fell until I caught you," Nessa said, but I knew she wanted to say more and couldn't.

Oh shit, that means she picked up on something when I so-called 'fell out and probably couldn't say it in front of Kim.

"So you ready to play?" Kim hissed, and it shot a cold chill up my spine, and I did what I could to ignore it.

I realized what I had to do, and that was trying to get all the robbers on one page as much as I possibly could.

Since I can remember each of their psychology, it does help a lot. Although I can't mention what I heard, I do know how to approach the situation because the fucked up thing is, I can relate to all of them, so I just have to put my fear aside and focus on getting us together.

Banding us together and making sure we get to be a unit is my priority right now, but that means I have to establish trust with them, and it may mean having to tell my dark secret to obtain their confidence, but it's only gonna be my last option. Not my first.

"So tell us the truth, are those guns real, or did you just wanna be a dickhead?!" Nick asked with a drunk chuckle, and I noticed how his brown hair looked shaggy and undone.

Shit, he's been drinking. That's not good.

"Sooo, does everyone know the rules?" Kim said, returning to her peppy demeanor.

My lip twitched in irritation because now I'm pissed that she's going to murder all of us without them knowing the plan but Nessa and me. Wait a second, I couldn't hear Nessa's thoughts when I got shot. Why? Is it because she's on my side? Then why did she let me die that time when she had the weapons to get them off of me?

No, I know why. It's because she isn't like me and would only look out for herself if it came down to it. She wouldn't be willing to expose herself because of me.

As soon as that answer hit me, I was okay with it, and it's why I couldn't be mad at her even if I wanted to because in this game, it's survival of the fittest, and cuz I know the rules, I won't hold it against her.

"So the cops are me, Lisa, Georgia, Liam, Oscar, Neil, William, and Todd. The rest of you are the Robbers. It was decided before we left for the trip, sooo sorry we can't change it," she said lightly.

Nessa leaned in and whispered, "When you passed out, there was blood coming from the back of your head," and I paled. Wait, what? So I really did die?

"Then what?" I accidentally said in Russian, "You speak my language?" She asked in return.

"Yeah, I learned it a long time ago, back when I was doing dirty work in my teenage years," I explained, still speaking Russian.

"I understand why you kept it a secret, and whatever happened in that alternate reality where I felt the blood from the back of your head, I'm sorry," she apologized, "and now I'm sorry for not believing you like I should have." I tried not to be too emotional over it cuz I could feel it rising inside of my chest.

"Hey! What are you two whispering about?!" William called to the both of us, and I wanted to bet that none knew any foreign languages, predominantly Russian. Why would they need to know?

"We weren't talking about anything of interest," I explained and waited to see their reactions.

"What language is that?"

"Sounds dope,"

"Duuuude, you speak other languages?!"

"Russian, Spanish, Portuguese, and Arabic," and I noticed Nessa paled when I confessed to the group, if she's smart, she'll put two and two together and why I never wanted to be put in situations like these ever again. It's why no one can ever know my real name.

Kim's eyes narrowed, and it was like she snarled at me, but I ignored it.

"Are you fuckin serious?! Say something in Arabic!" Henry bounced on his heels like a puppy.

I decided now would be a good time to build the team if I'm gonna get them to trust me and thwart Kim's plans to murder us all in these goddamn woods.

"Good evening Henry," I said with a warm smile on my lips, and I noticed all the elected 'cops' were nervous around me when I spoke the language fluently.

"Who are you?" Nessa asked me, "I'm sorry, I'm sworn to death never to tell," I told her the truth.

"You lied to me?"

"I lied because I don't want to see any more people die," I tried not to shout at her cuz I knew she was severely upset with me, and I didn't blame her.

I would be upset with me, too, especially if I trusted me and was blindsided by a somewhat truth to who I am and what I've actually been through in my past.

"Oh wow, I wonder what they're talking about?"

"Excuse me! You can't just ignore the rest of the group?" Courtney shouted.

"Says who?" I replied to Courtney in Portuguese, and she glared at me stunned, "what the fuck did you say?" she challenged.

"I said, says who?" I switched to Spanish.

"Damn, that's actually kinda sexy how you switch from one language to the other," Henry commented.

"I think I have a crush," Derek said.

"How come I never noticed her until now?" Nick said to himself.

"Because I wanted to stay hidden," I replied to Nick in Arabic, "translation, I wanted to stay hidden Nick," I explained.

"But what for?" Henry asked me, confused, and the rest just looked dumbfounded at me speaking in general, and I always hated having the spotlight on me, even though no matter how hard I tried in the course of my life.

Kim cleared her throat to return the attention back to her, and I went back to saying nothing while I could feel Nessa fuming beside me.

"So is anyone going to play or nah?"

"Oh shit yeah, how do we play?" Derek asked with a gleeful smile on his lips, but they won't be smiling for long.

"READY! SET! GO!" KIM shouted, and we all bolted further into the woods as the leaves rustled and twig crunched beneath my boots the harder I ran.

Their laughter filled the air as they all ran behind me, and the only one able to keep up was Nessa, "When were you going to tell me!" She shouted in Russian.

"I never planned to, I'm sorry," I shouted so she could hear me, "I need you to believe me," I said, and right when I did, a bullet fired in the distance.

Everyone stopped running, and when I turned around to face them, they all looked like they sobered up quickly and glared around the forest at each other, "Wait, that wasn't real, was it?" Jasmine shivered even though its cool outside.

"Dude, I know what real gunshots sound like, and that was a real bullet," Nick confirmed, and I noticed the expression in his dark brown eyes shift entirely.

"Oh my God, Nick! You're freaking me out! Stop it!" Courtney whined.

Then another shot thundered in the air, and Jasmine fell to the ground, "OH MY FUCKING GOD! I'M BLEEDING!" She shouted in agony.

I gritted my teeth and closed my eyes; goddamn you, Kim.

"Holy shit!" Derek shouted.

"What the fuck!" Henry said.

"Is she for real?" Courtney screeched.

Nessa pulled out her pistol, aimed, and fired back.

"WHAT THE FUCK! PUT THAT DAMN THING DOWN, OR YOU'RE GONNA KILL SOMEONE!" Nick shouted at Nessa.

"Oh my God, she's a fucking psycho!" Jasmine whined while holding onto her open wound with her bare hand.

The damn thing is gonna get infected if her stupid ass holds it with her bare hands!

I stormed to her, "Nessa, offer us some cover fire!"

"They're coming! We need to—" Nessa started to say, but another shot was fired, and I heard Courtney thud to the ground.

My heart sank to the pits, already knowing what had just happened.

They just killed their first victim. Goddammit! Yet again, I failed as a leader, and so I swallowed my tears and got my act together.

They all hollered, and I tore off part of my shirt, and since she was fighting me out of her hysteria, she kept trying to look over my shoulder, "Get off of me, you crazy bitch!"

"Shut the fuck up and listen to me, all of you,"

"Oh my God, Courtney is dead! What the fuck! What the fuck!" Derek shouted, and I didn't need to look behind me to hear the leaves rustle loud enough to know he was pacing back and forth.

"What the hell is happening!?"

Nessa fired more shots, and since she was in my field of view, I could see her holding her stance firmly while firing off her weapon in the direction of the shots.

"WHAT!? COURTNEY IS DEAD!" Jasmine shouted, and I noticed her tears fell, "No, there's no fucking way she's dead. Those are blank shots!" Jasmine kept trying to defend Kim.

I squeezed the cloth around her arm, and she screamed in pain, "You crazy bitch, this has something to do with you, doesn't it?!" She blamed.

"Red, they're getting closer, we have to move NOW cuz I don't have enough bullets to keep them off our asses!" Nessa reminded.

"Where the hell is Fox?" I asked one of them in a commanding voice, "I didn't see her here with us," Nick answered.

"Are you fucking kidding me?! This is a nightmare. This has to be some kinda nightmare!" Henry freaked, "DUDE, why aren't you freaking out!"

I finally stepped away from Jasmine and said nothing more to her cuz I knew she was too upset and fragile to keep moving forward. One thing I've learned also is to cut the dead weight in situations like these; even if I really do want to save her, she has to be willing to save herself to earn my trust.

"Seeing dead bodies ain't anything new for me, neither is hearing gunshots either," Nick confessed with a shoulder shrug.

"GUYS, WE GOTTA RUN NOW!" Nessa shouted, and as soon as she did, I bolted without waiting for any of them.

And I heard all of them running even if they were reluctant. Some were crying, many were complaining, the rest were praying, but me, Nessa, and Nick said nothing.

"Guys! I heard gunfire. What the fuck is going on?!" Fox shouted from a distance even though I couldn't see her or where the voice was coming from cuz of how dark it was outside.

"It's happening again Fox, please tell me you have some weapons like I asked you to bring," I hollered in return.

"You're fucking crazy! All of you are insane! This is your fault! It has to be your fault!" Jasmine kept shouting.

"Why the hell would Kim want to kill us? We haven't done anything!? What the fuck did we do to deserve this shit!?" Henry kept saying over and over again.

"I don't know what the hell is going on anymore, but I don't like it, I wanna go home, I want out of this shit,"

"Well, that's not gonna happen!" I heard Fox shout as she finally made her way to the group dressed like she was ready for combat and carried a bookbag and a duffel bag with her, but she moved with ease.

I stared at her, and my chest swelled with pride, and I can't say why, but I guess it was just the thought of knowing she finally trusts me and is willing to do what is necessary to make it out alive.

"Kim said this is a game, but not the kinda game where she's playing with fake guns, this shit is real, and they are trying to kill us," I explained.

"BUT WHY!?" Derek demanded.

"We're her friends," Jasmine sobbed.

"I thought we were friends. I thought that's why she invited me on this trip, someone please tell me what's going on. I'm so confused and scared. I think I literally pissed myself," Henry said, shivering.

"Get down!" I ordered, and they ducked right when another shot was fired.

I heard the group of girls' sadistic laughter fill the night air, and I slammed my fist into the ground.

"Red, I'm sorry I doubted you. You were right about Kim the whole time," Fox apologized to me, "It's okay, Fox, I'm not mad. I know how you feel despite how hard I've been on everyone,"

"Can someone PLEASE tell me what the fuck is going on!"

"I wanna go home,"

"Someone, please get me the fuck outta here!"

"Listen to me, Kim and her gang are out to kill us, okay? So I need you to get your head out of your asses and listen to me, Red or Nessa, so we can get out of this shit alive!" Fox argued.

"I'm out of bullets," Nessa answered.

"This whole thing is fucking CRAZY! Do you know how INSANE you sound right now?!"

"Guys, something tells me we were her first target practice," I said.

The thought hit me the longer I stared at a single worm crawling over the pile of leaves, and I can't say why, but something tells me this all ties into what happened to us in the woods, making it out when maybe—we weren't supposed to? Is that why Kim is targeting us?

"What the fuck are you talking about?" Nick finally chimed.

"Are you talking about?" Nessa said in Russian, "That's exactly what I'm saying. What if the whole operation in the woods with us was a test to see if she could pull it off in the first place? Otherwise, why would she be so insistent on wanting to know what happened in the woods?" I replied.

"Oh my God," Nessa finally pieced it together for herself, and it was like she went pale enough for me to see her in the dark.

"WHAT? What are you talking about, Red?" Fox demanded to know.

"I said what if what happened in the woods with us is—" I said but cut myself off because I didn't want them to think the reason they're in this situation is cuz of me, but I know Jasmine already believes so, and I can't change her mind on that.

Fox's eyes flinched, and her lip quivered, "you're not serious, are you?" she said like she was gonna cry and all I did was nod my head.

"It's the feeling I get," I replied.

She closed her eyes and grit her teeth, shivering, "mother fucker," and I think she came to the same conclusion as me, though I can't really discuss more with them while all the others were here with us.

"LISTEN, YOU BETTER START TALKING NOW!" Jasmine ordered one of us to tell her what we were talking about.

"You guys were always talking among each other, so you clearly know something we didn't or don't! Are you a part of their plan to play this fucked up game!" Nick demanded.

"Courtney is dead; she's fucking dead. What the fuck am I gonna tell her family? What am I gonna tell her older brother when he finds out?!" Derek shouted.

"What the fuck is happening? This has something to do with the three of you?! It has to be, none of this shit would've ever happened if—" Henry blamed us but didn't finish his sentence cuz more bullets went flying in our direction.

I could hear it pierce through the trees with each shot fired, and they all started shaking.

The bullets stopped firing, and I jumped from the ground to my feet, "Guys, we need to run, now!" I ordered and bolted further down the forest.

I heard Nessa and Fox catch up to me shortly afterward, and the others trudged behind me. They were super slow in comparison.

"I can't believe this is happening to me? What did I ever do to deserve this shit!?" Jasmine whined.

"I'm gonna fucking die in this place, I'm gonna die," Henry complained.

I stopped and waited to hear more shots fired, and nothing for a few seconds then turned to Fox where she stood with a stern expression on her face.

"Fox, you don't have any weapons do you?" I asked her, "No, I don't. Kim took them all," she said.

"I kept my pistol and knife on me," Nessa answered, "I only had enough room for a few knives since I figured you wouldn't be able to bring one," I smiled, reaching in my pockets and handed Fox a weapon.

She took it from my hands, flicked it open, then tucked it back inside, "Thanks, sis," she replied sincerely.

I nodded and said nothing else as me, Nessa and Fox turned to face the rest of the group, and they all looked mortified.

"Someone in this mother fucker better tell me what happened," Nick said sternly.

"Yeah, the hell is up with all of you and the secrets!?" Jasmine snapped.

"I say fuck them, and let's get out of here on our own!" Henry suggested.

"I just can't believe this shit is happening right now. I can't believe Courtney is actually dead," Derek shivered, crying.

"I'll tell them the truth, but right now, we have got to find a water source, same as last time, set up camp, and regroup since I'm assuming the camp we ran from is theirs. Nessa, make sure to use your knife to make marks towards the water source cuz if one of them comes after you solo, you can take them out with a blunt object or a dull knife if needed. So I want you to be the one to stay behind, and Fox, I want you to come back for the rest of us and lead all of us to the campsite. Wait till we come back to you cuz I have a few lighters which should help us get a fire going. Dismissed." I commanded.

"Got it," Nessa replied in Russian.

"I'm on it," Fox said, and they both ran into the woods until the darkness cloaked them out of my sight. God, please let my plan work again cuz now I have to get them to trust me; otherwise, this whole thing will fail again.

They needed someone to defend them if it ever came down to hand-to-hand combat since none of them had any idea what was going on.

"Who died and made you the boss all of a sudden?" Jasmine snapped.

"How did you know what to do?" Nick asked curiously.

"Why the fuck did they listen to you?!" Derek argued.

"Who the hell are you?" Henry asked, still trembling.

I took a deep breath and decided to tell them as much of the truth as I could without it meaning my life or theirs since they stopped firing shots, for now. I figured this would be as good a time as any.

I relaxed my expression, and when I met each of their terrified gazes, they all went pale, and Nick instinctively stepped away from me as if mortified by my glare.

"Why do your eyes look like that?" He said, trying not to shiver at the darkness in them.

Chapter 2: The Truth No One Wants To Hear

Tessa (Red) Parker

"It's cuz I have a lot of bodies on me that my eyes look like they do now," I answered honestly.

"What the fuck does that even mean!" Derek shouted.

Another shot was fired, and I ducked while, unfortunately, Derek got shot in his shoulder as the blood gushed out of his wound that ended up covering most of his arm.

"AH, SON OF A BITCH!" He shouted, and I didn't waste time reacting and doing the same with his wound, same as Jasmine.

"Get your filthy hands off of him!" Jasmine argued, trying to shoo me away, but since I was in this mode, I blinked, and when I opened my eyes, she was face-first into the dirt ground with me pinning her under me.

"GET OFF OF ME, YOU FUCKIN BITCH!" She shouted.

When the guys tried to get me off of her, I easily shoved hard enough for them to stumble onto their asses.

"I need you to calm down, please?" I asked sincerely, and she kept trying to break free of my grasp.

"Fuck you! This whole thing is cuz of you, isn't it!? So no, I ain't never gonna let you live this shit down! No fucking way! Get the hell off of me!"

"You wanna die or make it out of here alive?!" I argued with her pressing my knee in her back, and she screamed, "Owww my GAWD STOP IT! GET OFF OF ME!"

"Your friend Courtney is DEAD! This is not a game anymore," I snapped.

I was so over them bitching at this point.

"I've done a lot of fucked up shit for less, so PLEASE I am ASKING you to calm down and listen to me,"

"Are you threatening me! Wait till I get out of here and lock your ass up for assault and harassment!"

"It won't matter if your ass is dead!"

"Then I'll leave a letter saying you did it,"

"YOU WANNA DIE THAT BADLY!?" I shouted in her ear and pulled her arms back to cause her pain to understand how cruel this world is. It's better I cause her pain than them cuz they would laugh at her dead body, and it would actually hurt me to see her dead, just like Courtney.

"OH MY GOD, STOP! THAT FUCKING HURTS! GET OFF OF ME! STOP IT!" She sobbed, and I let go of her wrists until she slammed to the ground.

I stood up and turned to face the others behind me, "Jasmine listen, I'm sorry for hurting you, but I want you to understand; they don't care about you or you making it out alive. I'm asking you to trust me to get us all out of this alive," I asked sincerely.

"Why the fuck should we trust you!" Nick argued while dusting the dirt off of his shirt.

"Especially after you just tried to snap Jasmine's arms off!" Henry cowered in fear.

"But she did bandage my wound, though," Derek mentioned.

"And she bandaged my wound up too, so the fuck what! The bitch tried to suffocate me and then tried to rip my arms off! What kinda fuckin psycho does that!"

"You all want to be left here then?" I snapped.

The conversation grew quiet, "Cuz I don't need you to find their campsite. You'll be the ones stuck out here, with no food, no water, and no weapons, which makes each of you easy targets," I explained, so they understood how dire this situation is.

"They wouldn't leave us out here like that!" Jasmine argued.

"No, they wouldn't. This is still just some sick joke. It has to be," Henry said.

"But why would they? We have our own cabins, can't we just go back there?"

"If they planned this out the way I think they did, then no, they would expect you to go back there first and would more than likely have awful traps set up for us," I said plainly.

"BITCH, THIS ISN'T SOME FUCKING HORROR MOVIE! Shit like this DOESNT happen to people like me!" Jasmine defended.

I grabbed my last knife then tossed it on the ground.

"Then good luck," was all I said, turned, and started walking from them, and I did what I could to ignore the way my heart was sinking the further I strolled away.

None of them ran after me this time, and I don't blame them. Accepting the reality of this situation would be hard for anyone cuz it was for me back then too. I just hope they don't get targeted in the middle of the night, or they aren't stupid enough to try and go back to their cabins.

I silently prayed to myself that they would all make it out alive and decided to look for Nessa and Fox since we knew whats going on, and I knew now was the time to tell them the truth about me, again as best as I could.

I RAN INTO FOX, AND when our eyes met, "They're not coming, are they?"

"No, let's keep moving,"

"Yessir," she joked somberly, turned, and led me to the campsite.

Someone is gonna be dead again before sunrise, so I hope they have the will to fight.

I'm hoping Nick picked up the weapon seeing as he would make for a good leader if it ever came down to it. Since he said he's seen dead bodies and heard gunshots before, that's better than the other three. Henry is too scared, Jasmine is too full of herself, and Derek is just confused. My bet is on Nick if I had to pick one out of the group.

I met Nessa's glare, and she shot me a sad glare, "they couldn't trust you could they?" She said in Russian.

"No, I couldn't," I admitted with the same sadness in my voice.

This time I felt comfortable showing them my exhaustion as the leader cuz now I realize if I look human to them, it will regain their trust because the truth is I do care; I just know when to switch the 'not caring' aspect on when necessary. I hate myself for it.

I reached for my lighter and handed it to Nessa. She grabbed it from my hands gently and left to gather wood for us to start a fire since it's only getting darker the longer we stay out here, and I'm thirsty as all hell cuz it's hot out here.

So me and Fox spent the rest of the night catching our food and purifying the river water for all of us. Seeing all the stuff Fox brought made me want to cry; she had stashed away all of this from Kim even though she was staying with her, "I can't lie, sis, I almost brought this stuff in the cabin,"

"Where did you hide all of it?"

"Under the Cabin, I noticed the bus didn't leave, and when it didn't, I left these two bags on it, and then the next night when she was sleeping and totally sloshed, I hid it under the cabin in the cellar," she confessed, "it was just something about your warning I couldn't get out of my head no matter how many times I tried to fight with myself over it and you," Fox told me honestly.

Without warning, I grabbed her by the wrist and embraced her, "I'm so sorry I was hard on you, I was so damn scared you were gonna die first," I couldn't tell her all the visions I saw of her being the first to die among us as a group since I'd been away from them, so really Fox was the one I worried about the most.

"You really do care about all of us, don't you?" She asked, and I tried to squelch the emotions rising inside, "Yes, I do. I promise I do," I replied, needing to tell her the truth. The same goes for them, too, even if they don't know, can't see, or don't understand. I'm not angry or upset with them for not trusting me.

"I believe you. I'm just sorry it took till now for me to believe you," Fox apologized and hugged me back, and I couldn't stop my tears falling down my cheeks silently. I don't sob anymore like I used to.

"I never wanted to go back to this life, never, I couldn't stand losing any more people I love and care for because of my weakness as both a comrade and a leader," I shivered under the weight of how gentle her hug felt to me. I hadn't been hugged in a long ass time.

It's why I'm alone now because everyone dies cuz of me or lack of leadership. But like Fox, I wanted to be normal, and the longer I hold her, I realize I can never be normal like the rest of the world.

"Is that why you came to our school?" Fox asked as if stunned by my confession, "Yeah, it is, so I could try and not be like this," I said honestly.

"Goddamn, I'm sorry," Fox said and held me tighter.

The sincerity of her embrace to comfort me made it hard for me not to break under the weight of it. She has no idea what it took to get here where I don't sob when I cry anymore.

"I know this situation is shitty, and I hate it more than I care to admit, but when I heard those gunshots and screams, I realized first off that you were right, and then I remembered that since Kim told me it was a group activity, I couldn't help but think shit, what if other people are gonna be hunted like I was? And it was right then I made up my mind that I can do something about it and use what I know how to do and save someone else instead," Fox said while petting my hair like I was her little sister even if I'm older than her.

"So better me to see the shit than them, right? It's really no different than me not wanting my sister to ever see this side of me, and truthfully, they could too, right?" Fox consoled.

My tears fell harder, and I nodded calmly, "Thanks, Fox,"

"It's not much, but I gotcha back, whatever you decide from here on out, and yes, I'm still gonna bitch about it, but I'll do it, kay?"

I nodded, and when I broke from her, I wiped my tears, and Nessa sat beside us and glared at me, "I know how you feel, and it is why I will trust you same as it was back in the woods the first time despite what I think I know about you," she said in Russian.

My eyes met the leaves underneath us, and I nodded my head as the weight inside of my chest lifted at her words, "I'm sorry, Nessa, please forgive me," I genuinely asked.

Fox sat up from us and went to get another piece of fish cooking over the open fire, and Nessa rubbed my back to console me.

I smiled, as Nessa and I are cut from the same cloth regarding hardships, so we have the inherent understanding of some things other people wouldn't, so her rubbing my back was her way of saying, I forgive you, I trust you, and we're gonna make it out of this thing alive.

I could tell by her somber smile on her lips, and Nessa rarely smiles, if at all.

"All of you are important to me, so I can't let Kim win,"

"I think now is the time we finally hear what you saw about Kim regarding your vision about her and her mother," Nessa said in her language.

"What did Nessa say?" Fox asked me with a mouth full of fish with her eyes darting from one to the other, "I said I think it's time for her to tell us what she saw in her vision regarding Kim and her mother," Nessa translated.

"You know Russian?" Fox asked me, "Yeah, I know Russian, Spanish, Portuguese, and Arabic," I told her the truth.

"Dude, that's really fucking cool, but I think Nessa is right since there's no denying that Kim and those guys are hunting us right now," Fox smiled.

So I told them what I saw about the way she murdered her mother brutally in the chem lab, the way she dragged the knife down in her chest, and the way she gurgled a barely-there plea, and what she specifically said: "I knew I should've aborted you when I had the chance." Why would she say something like that?

Then I went into explaining what happened when there was blood oozing out from the back of my head while I passed out in Nessa's arms like what she said I did. So I told her what I saw and heard everyone's thoughts in my head before I died except hers.

"Oh my God, so you're telling me that stuff is real?" Fox said, tugging on the strings of her hoodie while Nessa lay on the ground staring at the open sky beside me.

"I don't know what the hell this is, and I damn sure don't know why every time I die or either one of you dies, I come back to life, but that's not the case with anyone else, I can't say why cuz I don't know,"

"Well, there's no denying that I felt and saw blood on my palm when you passed out in my arms," Nessa admitted cutting through the sounds of the forest, "then it was gone, and you woke up."

"This is some seriously freaky shit. What do you think it all means?" Fox said, letting go of the threads.

"Guys, if I'm honest, I really think Kim despises all of us and wants to change the structure of the way the school is run. Think about it, her mother was the first to change the dynamics by having rich kids and poor kids go to the same school together to try and bridge the gap, and now she got murdered for it by her daughter. Why would someone of power like that kill her own mother? And judging from the look in her eyes, her mother wasn't the first victim,"

"How can you tell?"

"Her eyes told me," I replied.

"I was there, I saw what she means. She has more bodies on her than she cares to admit to others and is good at playing likable, and it's a part of her trap to get others to trust her, same as she tried to do with me asking questions about my personal life," Nessa chimed while crumpling leaves in the palms of her hand.

"So it's like Kim is some illusion of safety and security for the other students, and it's why they trust her and not you," Fox said, "I get why, cuz I didn't trust you not wholly until I heard the gunshots go off and the shouting." She admitted with a heavy expression.

"It's cool sis, I wouldn't trust me either. I can be honest," I mentioned.

"But I do now, especially when I can help and do my part,"

"So, what should we do?" Nessa asked outright.

I fixed my eyes on the burning flame in front of me, "I have to do what I can to save as many as I can from this situation, and in the meantime, figure out a way to expose her real nature,"

"How do you do that?"

"Cut off her resources, band together, then make her confess so we can turn her in,"

"How would that work? She's got status and can easily say she's the one that's been the victim?" Nessa commented.

"She's right, she was the one who told me the lie that she saw her mother commit suicide and how it fucked her up, which is her way of playing victim so people can feel sorry for her,"

"That's why the saying goes, a wolf in sheep's clothing," I said out loud.

Then when I heard screaming in the distance, without thinking, I immediately grabbed my weapon in front of me and made a beeline for where the scream was coming from. I heard someone else's footsteps run with me, and I smiled.

We have to do what we can to protect them.

I would rather die doing the right thing, so my mind is made up. Thank you, Fox, thank you, Nessa, for staying by my side through all of it.

When we made it to where the screaming was coming from, I froze and saw Derek crawling away from a figure dressed in all black.

Nessa and I tucked ourselves behind the trees and waited for the right moment to strike. My heart plummeted when I saw Henry's corpse sprawled onto the ground, and I silently cursed myself for letting this shit happen. Nick was standing in a daze, unable to move or do anything, and Jasmine was sobbing uncontrollably northeast of me in the corner. They're all too shocked right now to do anything.

"Neil, seriously, please, this is crazy," He choked a sob.

Neil laughed at him, and he cried harder.

"Don't you fucking get it? YOU'RE OUR slaves, not the ones in charge, and WE are gonna remind you what happens—" Neil said, pointing the weapon at his head, "Now!" I commanded.

I leaped for Neil's back, then wrapped my arms around his neck while Nessa swiveled a kick towards his ankles. I used my weight to bring him down with me to expose his chest so Nessa could take him out.

Since he was in shock, he ended up firing the gun in the air aimlessly and started coughing and choking the harder I squeezed his neck, "Oh my God, please stop! I don't wanna die! This wasn't supposed to happen this way! Come on, I'm just another student like you!" He whined.

I hate people like him, the people that pick up a gun and think it's easy or cool to kill people, but when it's them, they run like a fucking coward. It sets me off. If you're gonna kill someone, you own that shit and don't run like a pussy. Cuz I didn't.

I blacked out, and all I heard were muffled screams before everything faded.

When I came back, I noticed Neil was suffocating me with his dead weight. Shit, I killed him by snapping his neck, goddammit.

I tried to push him off, and Nessa did what she could to get him off of me, and out of my contempt for his last words, I spit on him, "Pussy," I growled.

Nessa kicked his corpse, "I hate weak men," Nessa said in Russian, and I couldn't help but chuckle cuz she's just as fucked up as me, which is so not a good thing.

"You're fucking psychos, both of you are," Jasmine glared from her hands, shaking like a leaf.

I shot her a stern glare, "Well, we're the psychos that can get your ass out of here alive," I reminded, trying to climb out of the dark pit inside of my mind cuz right now I'm too pissed off at what Neil said to think straight.

The longer I'm in this shit, the easier it is for me to go back to the way I was, the way I never wanted to go back to.

"What about the bodies?" Nick asked us, "We can't worry about them right now, and I'm not saying it doesn't suck or it isn't right. Hell, none of this shit is right, but our main goal is getting our asses out alive more than anything, okay?" I said, a little more gentle than before.

"How the fuck are you guys so calm about this?! Two people are DEAD cuz of this shit! Then you tried to take Jasmine's arms off! THEN you killed

NEIL WHOSE OUR CLASSMATE! How can I trust you!? How the hell do you expect me to trust two fucking psychos!" Derek shouted, and I could tell his voice was hoarse and is beginning to suffer from mild dehydration.

"Well, I don't know about you, but I'm going with them," Nick replied to the other two, "You can't be serious. You can't just leave us here!" Derek complained.

"Besides, I want to know what she knows, and no, I'm not saying I trust her, but she is right about getting my ass out of here alive. I got a family to go back to, and while my conditions aren't ideal, they all I got in this world, so it's my family over you, and right now I choose my family," Nick affirmed.

"Where's the knife I tossed?" I asked, "I picked it up, but I couldn't do shit with it," Nick confessed.

"I'll admit I've seen some shit in my life, but nothing like this before,"

"How the hell did you just kill him so easily? Like it was nothing? You didn't hear his cries for his family? You didn't hear him call out for his girlfriend!? DOES NONE OF THAT MATTER TO YOU!" Jasmine shouted.

"In this game, we're playing none of that shit matters, but yes it does," and I carry the pain of each life I've ever taken, and it's why I don't sleep, if at all.

"Well, I can say this, I don't wanna die, not here, not like this," Derek said, wiping his tears, and finally stood up to join us.

"So you're all just gonna leave me here?! I'm a woman! I'm not supposed to be the one to get into this shit. I'm not supposed to be in this situation at all! YOU CAN'T leave me here!" She complained and sobbed.

I said nothing more to her, turned around, and started walking back to camp, following the markings we carved in the trees. She hollered for us to come back, and I got tired of her yelling, so I ran back to her and applied just enough pressure to knock her out so she would stop yelling and drawing attention to us.

"Nick carry her," I asked, and when I lifted her body off the ground, he threw her over his shoulder like she was a sack of potatoes; even if she doesn't wanna come with us, I'm not giving her a choice this time. She has to learn to face reality right now.

"Nessa, lead them to camp," I told her, and she nodded her head and left, "What are you gonna do?" Derek asked me.

"I just want to be alone with them if it's okay," I said to him.

"Why so you can make fun of them for being dead! You're really fucking sick," Derek cursed.

Then when I heard Derek coughing, I turned to look around and see Nessa flaring her nostrils at him, "Don't you get it, you fucking imbecile! She's paying her respects to those who've died here and is apologizing for not saving them when we could have. So shut the fuck up, and let's MOVE NOW!"

I could tell they all looked stunned, "But why? It's not her responsibility. She's not the leader!"

"She's a leader by knowing how to get our asses out alive, the same as Fox and me, none of you are trained for combat, and aren't used to these conditions, and because we ARE trained, it is OUR responsibility to protect those who are weaker than us. But if you were not so caught up in your own weaknesses, you would be able to recognize that in someone else," Nessa argued for me, and I returned my vision back to Neil and Henry's carcasses.

I knelt to Neil first, closed his eyes, and placed my hand on his sweaty forehead, saying nothing, and decided to pray instead. There is nothing eerier than feeling the warmth of someone after they've died, and it breaks something inside of me every time I do.

Now he is a part of me because I have taken his life and will see every aspect of his spirit in my nightmares just like everyone else I've ever killed in this life. Just once, I would love nothing more than to sleep peacefully and live peacefully.

"God forgive me," I asked, standing up from his carcass and did the same with Henry, "I'm sorry, Henry and Courtney," I apologized to them, trying to ignore the weight inside of my chest, and every time this happens, it's like the weight sinks so heavy it makes it hard to breathe. This pain is so intense my chest is both numb and suffocating at the same time, but I'm used to it by now.

They all kinda just stared at me, saying nothing.

"You're just doing this for show," Derek shouted, but I said nothing because the truth is, whenever I do have time, this is just how I've always been in times like these, but that's only when I have time. Otherwise, I pray for them at night, and it's not so I can get some sleep, it's just I want to forgive myself, but I can't, no matter how hard I try or how hard I pray.

But Fox is right, I have to do my part to make sure this shit doesn't keep happening, and now I realize I have to stop Kim at all costs, so I never have to look at the corpse of dead students who've barely gotten married or had kids or done any of the good stuff in life that's worth defending. Shit, I thought, trying to lodge the tears in my throat, and so I did.

I stood up from their dead bodies, and instead of joining or leading the group, I just walked past them, caught in my numb apathy back to camp.

I'm constantly reminded that I can't be both someone who prays for others and take life, that I can't be both caring and a killer. But all I can do is my best, cuz I know I'm flawed, but there's no point in trying to justify that to others as they wouldn't understand.

"Got nothing to say to us?" Derek kept saying, but I tuned him out, "Dude, shut the fuck up!" Nick argued.

Nick and Derek talked to each other the closer we got to camp, "Nessa, make sure to purify more water for them cuz I know they're thirsty, and see if we can catch more fish," I reminded.

"Got it," She answered.

I could feel both of their gazes on my back in confusion, "We have blankets by our camp, and while it's not gonna be comfortable, anything is better than nothing," I reassured, not turning to face them.

"Wait, so you guys KNEW this was coming!?" Nick asked me, "No, I didn't, I just had a strong hunch, and that's cuz I've always been suspicious of Kim, and it's why I told Nessa and Fox to pack a survival kit, and they did. But it's not because I knew," I told them the truth.

"You're lying! You knew the entire time they were gonna do this shit!" Derek accused.

"Well, whatever, they got the goods, and that's enough for me, especially after seeing Neil kill Henry point-blank until he pissed and shit himself with fear. Yeah, I just want nothing more than a hot ass meal, some water, pussy, and a way to pass out. To hell, if it's on the dirt, it's better than sleeping on the street corner," Nick answered to shut Derek up.

"Ew, seriously? None of this bothers you?"

"It's not that different from the streets forreal; the only difference is this is like some Saw or Hunger Games type shit, which if you asked me is even more fucked up," He said.

I froze, and my eyes bulged. Is that what she wants? Neil did say they are supposed to be the ones in charge. So did Kim hate what her mother was trying to do by merging the different classes together?!

Oh my God, so if we were the first, it would make sense that she would target us first as revenge because we weren't supposed to make it out the first time alive with our three pursuers.

So she killed her mother, so she could play leader, deceive everyone, and then what? Host these types of trial games as extra curriculum?! Somehow the thought of that possibly being the answer made my blood boil, but I said nothing and kept walking.

"What did you figure out?" Nessa asked me in Russian.

"I'm not too sure Nessa, I'm still trying to piece it all together, but when it makes a little more sense or when my hunch is strong enough, I'll let you know," I replied.

"It's about Kim, isn't it?" She said, "Hey, what the fuck are you two whispering about?!" Derek demanded to know.

"About your friend Kim, Derek, but since you don't trust me, there's no point in me telling you," I argued.

"What about her?" Derek kept pressing me for an answer, but once we made it to the camp, I ignored him and decided now would be a good time to get some more food and water for them.

They're not gonna believe me, but it's the truth, and I know the truth is the hardest pill to swallow, and it's why we spend our whole lives running from it cuz it's too damn painful to face.

Once we got settled, Nick decided to wake Jasmine up so she could drink some water we had purified for them, so they did and damn near choked on it when they finally had a sip. Yeah, they were suffering from mild dehydration.

"So you had all of this shit and was gonna hold out on us?" Derek snapped, "I mean, you guys are really fucked up," Jasmine agreed.

"Listen, if you wanna know what I think is going on, take it or leave it. It's up to you at this point. But remember the news when Kim's mother died?"

"Yeah, what about it?" Nick asked while trying not to salivate at the fish we had cooking over the open fire, "Well, Kim murdered her mother," I said flatly.

"How the fuck do you know that?" Derek mention.

"There's no fucking way she would do that!" Jasmine argued.

"Listen, I'm in the shit pit, yeah, but Kim killing her mother? That's a little far-fetched, even for you," Nick finalized.

"I said to believe what you want to, my job isn't to try and convince you, but so we can all get out of here, I'm going to make her tell the truth, and it starts by cutting off her resources, corner her, and then make her confess the truth. And I won't stop until I do," I affirmed.

They all stared at me like I lost my shit, but I'm used to that feeling by now.

Nessa and Fox said nothing, then grabbed the stick with the fishes on it, served it, and gave it to the other three, and since the air was filled with spices from the fish, they snatched it and started gnawing on it like starved animals.

"Oh my God, why is this so damn good?!" Jasmine groaned, "No kidding," Derek moaned in satisfaction.

"I don't even eat fish, but damn, this shit is good," Nick answered.

It made me smile at the sight of them eating and knowing they are okay overall.

"Hey, I know your bat shit crazy, but why did you come back for us when you could've ignored any of us screaming?" Nick asked.

"I don't want to see any more of us die," I answered thoughtfully and looked at each of them, "Why do you care?" Jasmine demanded.

"I've seen some shit in my life Jasmine, and it's for my own selfish reasons I want you all to live and live a normal life and forget about this kinda shit. I realize now this is where I belong, and it's not with normal people. So yes, all of you were right, I'm not a normal person, and I tried. I really fucking tried, and that's the God's honest truth," I said.

Fox and Nessa's heads met the ground, and I knew they understood exactly what I meant.

"So then what about you two? Why do you believe her? I wanna know why you trust her?" Nick pressed.

"She saved our asses back when we got lost in the woods the first time, so really, we owe her our lives," Fox answered.

"I trust her because she is my friend and has risked her life on more than one occasion for me," Nessa told the truth.

"Did she not save you, Derek?" Nessa asked, turning to face where he sat to the right of me.

"She really did all of that?" Nick blinked, confused where he sat in front of me since we all sat around in a circle in front of the fire.

They both nodded their heads, "I'm alive because of her," Fox said.

"Are you saying she's willing to do the same for us? She barely knows us. At least she knew you guys beforehand!"

"Only for a few months before," Fox corrected.

I could tell they looked stunned when she said that to them, and it's true; I had only known them for a couple of months before shit hit the fan. But that didn't matter to me.

"Ayo, is that true?" Derek said, stunned, "No fucking way! The bitch tried to rip my arms off!" Jasmine fussed.

"I only did that because you refuse to understand the situation we're in, and your mentality is going to get us ALL killed," I explained.

"Well bitch, I don't HAVE to understand or agree with any of this shit if I don't want to; it's called MY freedom of speech,"

"And who the fuck you think died for your right and refusal to accept what's happening right now?! Courtney and Henry, that's who, so spare me the bullshit denial right now," I argued.

Then the space fell silent again where only the forest animals could be heard, crickets and owls hooting in the distance.

"You did save me," Derek reluctantly admitted, "You're welcome," I replied with a sarcastic chuckle.

Nick's light brown eyes met mine, and it had been a long time since my chest fluttered at the sight of a man. Ew, no, now is NOT the time for this at all.

"I've decided to trust you cuz I can tell they not lyin, so if what they sayin is true, I ain't got shit else to lose other than to die in this place, or by you, and forreal, either don't sound too bad at the moment," he smirked.

"Haha, very funny," I replied, and I made the mistake of having our eyes lock for too long before returning to my solemn glare back towards the group.

"Are you flirting with her, dude?!" Derek said in disgust, "Maybe, I've always had a thing for tough women despite everything that happened,"

"And who died and made YOU Alpha all of a sudden!?" Jasmine argued with the same disgust as Derek, "Last I checked, I did say I've seen a dead body before, and none of you have, sooo I'd like to think I qualify for the job,"

"Do you know how to fight?" I asked him.

"Wanna find out?" Nick challenged, and I knew he was officially flirting with me, "I don't see why not," I said casually.

I decided to drink more water and tossed him another water bottle so he could drink to prevent dehydration since we would be fighting.

"I'll go prep more water since you might be getting all sweaty in more ways than one," Nessa teased in Russian, knowing only I would've heard her.

"Oh, shut the fuck up!" I replied with a smile in Russian.

"The fact you speak multiple languages is low-key kinda sexy," Nick said after gulping down his water, and not gonna lie, I'm itching for a good fight.

"Well, I'm glad you think so; I needed to remember it for work," I said in Arabic.

"I have no idea what you said," He said, taking off the hoodie and tossing it to the ground, then and waited for me to meet him on the opposite side of the dirt we had cleared for our brawl.

"So if I win, we fuck," He said with a grin on his lips, "ew, why the psycho?" Derek asked, genuinely confused by his attraction to me.

I readied my stance, "and if I win, we don't," I replied.

"That's not gonna stop me either way, just delay me for a bit," He laughed, "cuz at the end of the day, pussy is pussy, and I've heard the crazier the bitch is, the better," he said with a light snicker.

I couldn't help but laugh, it was so refreshing for once to meet an honest dude who wasn't bullshitting me with fake ass lines and said how he really felt about me, and it was just to get laid.

And what's even more fucked up, I think that was when I found him the sexiest, but I have a thing for toxic, brutally honest men.

"How can you think of fucking at a time like this?"

"Cuz its a possibility I might die in this shit, so I might as well fuck before I die,"

"Good thing I brought those (condoms) too," Fox laughed, and I shot her a blank stare, "you ain't shit."

She beamed and giggled, "I know."

"Brought what?" Nessa asked, getting back to camp with more water, "Nothing," I replied firmly, trying not to be embarrassed by what Fox said.

"Fox, be useful and stand guard. You're on first shift this time since it was me the first time," I ordered, "Yes, ma'am!" she laughed, grabbing her knife and walked in the direction we came from.

"I got second shift," Nessa replied, "Good, get some rest in the meantime,"

"Damn you, giving orders is a lot sexier now that I can actually see your face since you spent most of this trip staying hidden in the cabin, and the fact they actually listen to you is even hotter than anything I've ever seen from a woman before," Nick flirted.

"Well, it won't matter since I'm winning this fight anyways,"

"Ugh, I'm gonna go sit by the water and contemplate drowning in it," Derek said, "Wait, I'm coming with you," Jasmine agreed.

Once I had relaxed my core and focused my breathing, I lurched for him, and our duel started.

Chapter 3: The Price of Being The Leader
Tessa (Red) Parker

I don't know how we ended up where we did, but since everyone was partnered up with someone, Jasmine and Derek, Fox and Nessa & I think they did that on purpose cuz they thought it would be a good idea for me to spend the night with someone else, not them, i.,e. with Nick.

I guess they are right cuz I damn sure could use the masculine energy right now.

After I had finished setting up my blanket on the ground, I used my hoodie as the pillow and went to lay down while ignoring all the sticks and leaves poking me in my side. I'm used to it.

"I know I said I would trust you, but I wanna know the truth," he said, laying beside me, but he laid close enough for me to tell he's there without actually touching me, which was a good sign for me right now.

"The truth about what, Nick?" I said, not turning to look at him and kept my eyes fixed to the open sky since it's the only sight giving me any comfort in this situation. I tried not to think of all the times I laid with my comrades glaring at the same sky, talking about what life would be like when we stopped working, and suddenly the thought made the tears fall silently from the sides of my eyes.

I didn't bother wiping them since I didn't want him to know I was crying.

"Like why you're crying, for example, I knew you weren't as much as a hard-ass as you were earlier," he said more as a joke than anything, but again, I don't easily trigger, not anymore.

I'm used to pain.

"I'm sworn to secrecy to never speak about my past, and so I won't. I don't want to see any more people die, Nick," was all I said as tears fell harder from my eyes.

He was quiet for a moment, "So then why are you crying?" He asked sincerely.

"I'm crying for the dead people," I answered.

"You're really vague, you know that, and I already know this is why no one could ever date you forreal,"

"Good, it should stay that way," I replied earnestly, "wait, I was joking. You're serious?"

I turned to face him, and when I met his green eyes against his dark skin, I followed my instincts and cupped his cheek in my hand; his eyes are so innocent compared to mine, I thought, and instead of backing away like I thought he would he just locked his eyes with mine.

"Look, if we're gonna fuck, let's just do it and get it over with, there's no reason for you to get involved with me by asking questions like that. Cuz the truth is, at the end of the day, I meant it when I said I can't have any more people die," I paused and tenderly rubbed my thumb against his cheek, "I'm. Tired." I emphasized as another numb tear trickled from my eye into my hairline.

"Ay listen, I know I said we was finna fuck sure, but if I'm trusting you with my life, I got questions," he said, pausing and putting his hand on top of mine. The warmth of his hand jolted up my spine, and another tear fell, "But the longer I do look at you, I can see you're not bullshitting me about not wanting to see any more people die. I just wanna know why."

The scruff of his dark beard against my palm was comforting to me, "people have died because of me, and I have done this before. Meaning I'm accustomed to this type of lifestyle, and that's all I can say to it," was all I told him.

"Your hands are calloused and weighty," he said to me, and I smiled, saying nothing.

"And your eyes are dark, which means you got some massive bodies on you, no thanks to my brother being the crazy one who's dead," he said.

I chuckled sarcastically and removed my hand from his cheek, then turned over and got a sip of water from my water bottle.

He said nothing and wrapped his arm around my waist, then tucked me into his core. The warmth of him against my back made me smile, "I've fucked a lot of girls, but you're insane," he whispered in my ear, and the vibration of his voice shot a jolt up my spine.

Then turned me over on my back and looked at me, "but so am I. I'm just better at hiding it than you," He gleamed.

Then kissed me hard. God, it had been for fucking ever since I kissed anyone cuz I don't kiss anymore. Maybe it's just my exhaustion, or perhaps it's my throbbing pussy at the moment, but when his lips met mine and the stubble of his mustache rubbed against my top lip, I shivered a moan in his mouth.

"Damn, I really wanted to kiss you," He groaned in my lips, and oh my fucking God, he's a good kisser.

I smiled in his lips, "Let me guess you're gonna say something like my lips are the sweetest you've ever tasted?"

He bit my bottom lip, and I trembled, "No, more like the deadliest poison I could never stop drinking cuz I'm addicted to death," and winked at me.

"Now that's sexy," I moaned.

We kissed, and I ran my fingers in his oily hair, but I didn't mind the slickness of it, anything dirty seemed masculine to me, and I damn sure craved it more than anything the longer our tongues are swirling in each other's mouths.

Before I knew it, we were fuckin, and this time it didn't go by like a blur. I didn't have to blackout my memory like all the other times.

I didn't feel violated or like I just wasn't in it like usual. It's weird with him; I was wholly immersed, and it was mind-blowing for me. I had never met a man who, even in outside (were about to die at any time) conditions, solely wanted to please me and didn't think of anything else BUT that moment with me.

I've literally faked sex most of the time, except one other time. Once, and with Nick, it'll be my second time I haven't had to fake anything.

The fucked up thing is, he could tell and got cocky in the middle of it, which I don't know how it ended up turning into an 'I will out fuck you' duel, but it was damn sure the fun release I needed same as him.

After we cleaned up, I heard the rest of the group murmuring among each other, and I did what I could to ignore it and got dressed.

I laid on my side and thought about the sex I just had, and damn, was it worth it. But I know I have to cut this shit off with him; otherwise, if he dies, it's only going to hurt me more than before. I hate being this way.

When he laid beside me and got under the blanket, "Damn girl, you got that WAP! (Wet Ass Pussy)" He joked, pinching the sides of my waist, and I swatted his hand away, "Go to bed, sir," I laughed.

"Listen, I know we can die at any moment in this shit, and I know we just fucked and don't really know each other, but it's different when I look at you, and cuz of that WAP you got," He ended with a joke.

"Get the hell away from me," I giggled.

"Oh Nah, not when you was moaning my name a few seconds ago, and legit you say it the sexiest," and started to imitate me saying his name during sex.

My face got so hot I punched him in the center of his chest and then buried my face in it right after to hide my blush.

"Oh, shit, are you blushing?" He laughed, "You're a dick," I mumbled in his chest.

The smell of his skin I just tasted not long ago gave me so much comfort. It was nice to be held, even if only for a second.

I broke from his embrace, then laid on my back and grabbed my weapon to keep it close to me in case anyone tried to ambush us.

"You don't sleep at all, do you?" He said.

"Nope, not really, and yes, I'm exhausted," I answered.

"Well, I think Fox was still on first shift, and Nessa has second shift, so you can relax," he said.

"I wish there are more of them and less of us, so we're sitting ducks and only have one gun among us, and the rest have knives, and last I checked, only three out of seven people know how to use any of these weapons, to begin with," I explained why I can't entirely relax even though I want nothing more than to pass out.

"Well, then sleep for as long as you can before the nightmares haunt you aiight," he said.

"Your brother?" I asked where I laid in his chest, and he wrapped his arm around me, "Yup," was all he said.

I finally conked out, and even though it was only for an hour, that hour of sleep was the lifetime of peace I craved in my slumber, and I finally had it without nightmares of all their faces, the blood, and screams of agony. And I didn't wake up in the middle of it sobbing uncontrollably alone.

WHEN THE NIGHTMARES finally came, I don't remember what happened, but I can say I felt his arms wrap around me, and it calmed me down when he tucked me in his chest.

"Ay ay, it's cool, chill, you're okay," he whispered in my hair, and I trembled, not realizing I was holding onto him for dear life, "Shit, I'm sorry," I apologized in Arabic since it was where my nightmare took place.

He rubbed my back and planted gentle kisses in my hair until my breathing returned to normal, and I reminded myself of where I am, "I'm okay," I lied, backing away from him.

I hated feeling this vulnerable.

"You good?" He asked in a low whisper not to alarm anyone else that was sleeping, but before I knew it, Nessa had rushed over and stood in front of me, "Are you okay?" She asked me in Russian.

"Yeah, I'm okay, just another nightmare," I told her honestly cuz I knew she would understand what I was going through.

She hardened her glare and nodded her head, saying nothing and didn't give me words of comfort since it wouldn't mean much, to begin with. Maybe seeing Nick being so affectionate with me is the other reason she backed off too, but I'm still not sure.

I can't believe one night of passionate sex, and now he's all over me, wanting to take care of me and shit, and as much as I tried to run, I couldn't, not really.

I glared up at the sky and noticed the sky started to turn light blue, "Nessa, get some rest. I'll take over the final shift since I slept," I said. Then stood up from Nicks's arms and strolled towards Nessa, and she handed me the weapon we took from Neil's corpse since this and knives were our only form of defense against them if they tried to attack all of us while we're sleeping.

Now is the time for me to plan our next move, and I needed to do it alone, away from Nick, and process my feelings about him since I can't get too attached in case he dies, cuz all its gonna do is scar me like everything else in my life.

I held the gun to my chest, quickly scanned the area, and closed my eyes to listen to the sounds of nature and see if they could be anywhere nearby, and still nothing. Maybe they're trying to strike us again like last time. So whose left? Kim, Lisa, Georgia, Liam, Oscar, William, and Todd. So there are seven of them and six of us. Shit, the odds aren't good.

"Ayo, how we gonna bathe?" Nick joked, standing by my side, and I smirked, "ask if Fox brought soap, cuz I'm sure she did," I answered.

"Bet," He replied, and when I turned around, I noticed Fox was awake by the river getting more water to purify for everyone to pack for the day while trying to get food.

I know all of us are exhausted, and the rest are sleeping like logs. Deadweight is what we call Jasmine and Derek to people like me, and there's nothing more dangerous than carrying around dead weight.

The only other person whose helpful in this situation is Nick. At least he knows how to fight, which is a good sign, even if he did lose to me. Then I saw Nick kick Derek in the back, and Derek groaned awake, "what the fuck is your problem, dude!?" he shouted.

"Getcha ass up!" He argued, "ain't nothing more disgraceful than a man that sleeps while the women doin all the work. That's no different than letting my sisters take care of me. Don't you got any fuckin shame, bro?" He said.

I smiled and returned my sights to the barely lit forest in front of me, listening to the sounds of nature. It oddly soothed me since nature was my training grounds since I lived in it for months when I was training back then. I also trained in the snow, and that shit sucked more than anything, but I do know since it's humid out here, the air is only gonna dehydrate us, so I hope Fox made enough water for everyone to carry for the day. We're gonna need it.

"Just cuz you got some pussy doesn't mean you got the right to boss me around! I swear when this shit is over, I'm reporting all of you for this mess!" Derek complained.

I don't blame him. This situation would be challenging for anyone to deal with, mainly civilians. It's the other reason I can only get but so mad, but Jasmine specifically pisses me off cuz she keeps thinking she has power even in this situation when she fails to realize she doesn't. In this type of world, no one gives a shit about money, status, and title. Death don't take MasterCard.

"Nick, check their wounds and make sure it's not infected," I ordered without turning around, "aiight," was all he replied.

I heard Fox step beside me and look out into the forest with me, "sis, I got water for all of us," she reminded me.

"Thanks, girl," I said sincerely, "did you get enough sleep?"

"Yeah, for the most part, but it's hard for me not to be paranoid in this kinda shit, ya know?"

"You holding up, okay?" I asked, wanting to make sure as I turned around to face her and I noticed her expression was more sunken than before, "not really, but I got no choice, right? I got people I wanna protect. Whose families I want them to get back to," she replied.

"It's funny, knowing Nessa, she would be cruel enough and say just kill Derek and Jasmine since their dead weight to us," I mentioned.

"That's so fucked up, but I think I get it," Fox smiled.

I returned my view back to the forest and held the gun close to my chest.

"They're an endangerment to the rest of us because they cannot and will not adjust, and one of us can die because of it," I said, needing to tell her the truth of our situation because of them. We are gonna be slowed down because of them not reacting fast enough and our need to protect them, which also limits my capabilities in combat.

Fox was quiet for a minute before saying anything, and the sounds of a forest animal bellowed in the distance.

"I made my peace with that last night, sis," Fox replied somberly.

I breathed an all-knowing sigh. I know exactly what she means.

"The thing is, none of us are good people, especially not me, and as much as I'm willing to fight and make it back to my family, I would rather die protecting someone than just being scared and not doing shit about it. Remembering the way I killed Adam reminded me of that," she said.

"You're right. None of us are good people, and I know I'm going to hell when this is all over," I admitted.

She bumped my shoulder with hers, "you have no one and nothing to go back to, do you?"

"No, I don't, so if I die, I'm more than okay with it. You, on the other hand, need to make it out of this shit alive. You have a future, Nessa has a husband, and I know everyone else has families to get back to, whereas, with me, I got no one to make it back to,"

"Well, what about you and Nick? I know the shit is new and all, but it sounded like last night was totally worth it," Fox joked.

I laughed, "Nah, he's got a life back at home and a family to protect. He's the man of his household, I saw it in my vision before I died the second time,"

"You never talked about that, did you?" Fox mentioned with curiosity.

"The thing is, I was able to understand why each of them fought me at every point, and it's thanks to my vision before I died a second time. Lisa's been molested by her dad, and Oscar was also sexually abused, and Kim helped them. Jasmine and Todd need Kim to be popular and move up the ranks. William and Neil were the racists and hated people of color like me, you, Derek, and Jasmine. Derek is bi-sexual and needs a place to belong, and it's why he defends Kim, and even with Nick, Kim helped him, so he didn't have to sell and deal drugs anymore to take care of his mom and sisters. He doesn't wanna be the deadbeat dad like his father was to him and his sisters. Courtney was afraid of being poor and would've done anything to keep her status, and Henry was afraid to be alone," I said, "So them dying means they can never accomplish those goals, or see them come true, or see them grow from their pain."

My expression remained even, but I felt the tears well in my eyes since I feel nothing when I talk about stuff like this. I didn't have to look at Fox to know she was dumbfounded by what I said about each of them, "And you are like me. You just wanted to be normal and not some monster capable of taking lives. I'll be honest, this is the reason I was the hardest on you back then, and for that, I'm sorry," I apologized to her finally.

"Damn, sis, you've carried all of this alone and never told anyone?" Fox asked with shock and a tinge of pain in her voice, "Nope, I see no reason to," I replied.

"How the hell do you know that?" Nick asked from behind us, but instead of being shocked, I said nothing in return.

"It's a gift she has, and it's how she knew about this whole thing going down with Kim in the woods," Fox explained plainly.

"I don't believe that shit. What else do you know about me?" Nick demanded sternly.

"Other than what I said, Nick, nothing else. But it's the reason I'm not mad or angry for the most part, except for Jasmine. She pisses me off to no end," I said, trying to memorize where the trees were in front of me.

"So you know about my sisters and my mom? You knew I was dealing drugs and shit in the streets? No one was ever supposed to know about that shit, and you knew? What did you do, look up a file on all of us or what?"

"Believe what you want, Nick, like I said to you last night, I'm tired," was all I said in return.

"Why the hell do you make it so hard for any of us to believe you?" Nick argued.

"Hey, you better back the fuck up, homeboy," Fox said, "Guys enough," I commanded in my leader's voice.

"Fox is telling the truth, I died twice, and I came back to life, I can't explain it, I don't know how, and I damn sure don't have the time to try and figure that shit out. And it's not that I'm keeping secrets; I just can't expect any of you to understand."

"That's my problem," He said, stomping in front and glared down at me, "you expect all of us to trust you, when you won't even be honest with us and how you KNOW all of this shit about this entire situation, and now about us,"

"Nick, I AM being honest, but one thing I know about people is that as long as it does not align with their beliefs, human beings will ALWAYS reject what does not work for them, and its the other reason why I don't wanna argue or fight with anyone anymore," Even if I do still want to save everyone from this shit in the first place. I can't do it alone.

"You wanna know the truth!? Fine, then tell everyone to get their asses over here, and I'll finally tell the truth since you want to know every goddamn thing!" I argued, and I usually don't get this emotional, but I'm tired of everyone thinking I have all the answers when I don't.

So he did, except for Nessa, where we all stood huddled around each other.

"Back when me, Nessa, and Fox were stranded in the woods, three of our classmates were hunting us to the death, same as this shit now, but if I had to put two and two together, my guess is Kim set this up the first time, and we were not supposed to make it out alive. It's the other reason she's specifically targeting me, Fox and Nessa making it a point to get closer to them and try and put them against me," I paused. All of them scrunched their faces in disapproval, "then I had a vision of Kim murdering her own mother when I got back from the woods." And I let my words hang in the air for a moment, knowing they were gonna fuss me out.

"There's no fucking way that happened," Derek rejected, "You really are fucking crazy," Jasmine blamed. But Nick said nothing and kept listening to what I had to say.

"After that vision I had, I wanted to verify it for myself, so when I went to see her for a counseling session, she was really adamant about wanting to know what happened in the woods with me, Nessa, and Fox cuz I told them not to spill what happened to us and turns out my suspicions were right about her. Next thing I know, I damn near pleaded with Nessa and Fox to bring a survival kit just in case and to be prepared for this next trial. Once we got here, this is the same woods we made it out of the first time, and once I knew that, I knew she was going to put us through this trial, but I still couldn't be sure until last night when she announced were gonna be playing Cops and Robbers, the kill or be killed version," I finally explained.

"So you're telling me you knew all of this without actually know knowing?" Nick said in disbelief, "Yes, when we came back from the woods the first time and made it to the school, I saw Nessa, Fox, and me die. Next thing I know, I'm reaching for Fox and trying to tell her ass to calm down, so we don't set off the security officer who almost tased me on my way to the cafeteria to hang out with them."

"Nick, we fucked, so you've seen my scars. I figured out those scars are not just mine from my past but also from when I died. Didn't you feel an odd knot on the back of my head? The next vision I had at the campfire was when I heard everyone's thoughts about Kim and why each of you rejected me telling the truth about her and laughed when I got shot in the head by Neil," I said dead serious.

They all stared at me blankly, Derek had his mouth open, and Jasmine looked conflicted, like she was fighting with herself to believe me.

Nick looked like he was gonna burst out in a fit of teary-eyed rage at me, telling them all the truth finally.

"Listen, I didn't believe her and fought her at each turn, only to realize her gift is the reason my ass is alive, so while I don't expect you to believe her, I do and trust her with my life from here on out," Fox remarked firmly to the group.

"And hey, sorry for using you as bait," I joked, "Nah, it's all good; scars make me look cool now," and we fist-bumped.

"Wait, you USED HER AS BAIT!" Jasmine shrieked.

"How fucked up are you?" Derek said, appalled.

"So you do what's necessary to survive, right?" Nick asked, gazing directly into me and not at me, "Yes, and will do so for all of us to make it out of here," I reaffirmed.

Gunshots roared through the air as me, Fox, and Nick all ducked in time to miss the bullet, but Derek was hit again and landed on the ground, "Oh son of a bitch! Why am I always the one that gets shot!" He groaned in agony, kicking and screaming.

"Cuz you don't react fast enough!" I argued.

"Okay, miss know it all! What the fuck are we supposed to do now!" Jasmine shouted, and I stayed crouched and aimed my weapon into the woods but saw no one. Shit, what if they're in the trees? Oh God, no! It means they have the advantage not just in numbers but also in firearm power and the lay of the land. Mother fucker.

I aimed at the trees above and spotted one of them dressed in black and noted the distinct blonde hair, "RUN YOU UGLY FUCKING MONKEYS!" William shouted.

I took a deep breath, tensed my muscles, and fired a few shots. Another one down, I thought, when he fell from the trees and dangled from the branches limp.

"Fox! Get his gun NOW!" I ordered, and she darted for the weapon, "Nick, I need you to lead them further down the stream, stay low to the ground, grab as much of our shit as you can until you get to a safe spot and tend to Dereks wound. I need all of you to make it out of this shit alive. I'm so fuckin serious!" I reminded.

Jasmine's expression paled as if it finally hit her when more pellets were fired in our direction; she didn't bother with ducking, "oh my God, you've been telling us the truth the entire time?"

"YES, NOW GET THE FUCK OUTTA HERE! NICK TAKE THE WEAPON FROM FOX! Do NOT hesitate to kill any of them if they shoot at you!" I commanded, aiming my weapon to the trees above, looking for more of them.

Fox stayed low and handed Nick the gun, "do what she says and get the fuck outta here NOW!" She said as he snatched the weapon from her and loaded the bullets in the chamber.

"Tessa," Nick said, aiming the weapon in the trees like me, "Make it out of this shit alive so I can fuck you again!" He said.

"Seriously, you still have time to joke at a time like this?!" Fox said.

Nessa finally joined up with us and crouched to the ground, saying nothing.

More shots were fired, and it hit Nick in his torso, "Ah son of a bitch!" He shouted.

"Don't bother wasting our bullets!" Nessa shouted.

"Fuck this!" Derek said, limping towards the river, and Jasmine followed after him, "God, I fucking hate you and this bullshit! UGH! I'm SO OVER IT!" She shouted.

In a quick moment, I felt Nicks's lips against mine in a quick kiss, and with that, I saw him bolt to the rest of the group holding his wound to stop the bleeding.

"Fox, go with them. Me and Nessa got this!" I said calmly, looking for the rest of our attackers in the woods, but only shots were fired, and it was hard for me to find the direction of where the bullets were coming from, goddammit.

"Worried about lover boy? Ok, sis, got it!" Fox joked but ran towards them with her knife in hand and quickly did what she could to pack the camp, tossed some water bottles in our direction, and since our resources are all we have, it's damn sure worth defending.

Nessa stood with her knife in hand, "Nessa, go scout the area and stay low to the ground. Take them out with your knife if you have to," I said.

She nodded her head and did as I told her, moving swiftly in between the trees, and it was like she dodged bullets, but I know that has more to do with her frame being able to move the way she does.

I decided to give her some cover fire until I felt something warm and sticky running down the side of my torso, and then searing pain hit me out of nowhere. Shit, I've been hit.

I fell to my knees and my eyes teared up from the burning pain. The blood gushing out of my wound made me dizzy, but I gritted my teeth and aimed my weapon, waiting for another one to expose themselves. I won't let Nessa die cuz of this bullshit wound. They're gonna have to earn my life.

So I stood up and followed behind Nessa, ignoring the blood that covered the side of my jeans and thigh, fuck I hate blood and how it sticks like muddy glue.

"HELL YEAH! I GOT ANOTHER ONE OF THEM SONS OF BITCHES!" I heard Liam shout in the distance, so I flexed my core and let my tears of pain fall from my cheeks, then aimed my weapon in the direction I heard him.

"THIS IS OUR TURF AND OUR SCHOOL! NOT YOURS!" And another bullet was fired from above as it hit my shoulder.

I hollered, "GODDAMMIT!" As more searing pain throbbed from the open wound in my flesh.

I got nothing to live for anyway, so I might as well bait them while Nessa sneaks up on them and takes them out. Then more shouting, caws and jeers from the sky until I paled when I saw a big ass bear in front of me growl.

I took my gun and fired in the center of its chest as it ran for me, but I stood my ground and didn't run. If I'm gonna die, I might as well face it and all the pain, even if it's gonna hurt like hell to die like this.

Right before it made its way to me, I didn't back away further enough, so its claws swiped the side of my cheek, and more blood gushed down my neck. I made sure to close my eyes when it happened cuz if blood gets in my eye, I'll be blinded and can't shoot like I need to.

Then it fell with a thud to the ground before bellowing in its last dying moments.

Goddammit, this shit hurts, and the salt from my tears stung my open wound, then my legs started to buckle, and dizziness was setting in the more blood spurted from my injuries.

So I mustered my strength and finally caught sight of Liam in the trees above me, took a deep breath, and fired at him, "OH FUCK!" He shouted before falling down the tree and landed on the ground with a thunk, dead.

"Ah, mother fucker," I grimaced, falling to the ground since my muscles were slowly starting to wane in function. No, I can't go out like this. Keep moving.

I did what I could to stand up, but my legs kept shaking, and the trees started to spin around me, and something told me this time, if I die, I'm not coming back to life. So I have to get this shit right and make it out alive. Even my only reason to live is for my fallen comrades.

Five targets left. Just five more targets, and hopefully, everyone makes it out of this shit alive. Then I'll be the one to sacrifice myself if necessary. I'm sorry, guys.

God, if I die this time, as much as I want redemption for my sins, I thought getting my legs under control as best as I could while shutting off the throbbing pain then stepped forward while aiming my gun at the trees; please let me meet my fallen comrades this time.

Then spotted Todd aiming his gun at me, but I fired first before he had a chance to shoot me, and he slumped in the tree with more blood running down the sides of the trunk.

Three more to go.

Then I heard Lisa shout to the top of her lungs in pain. Two more to go.

Where the hell could Kim and Georgia be? They would have to be back at the cabin watching this shit on their phones, or on cameras or some shit.

The bullets stopped, and once my adrenaline stopped, the pain washed over my body, and I stumbled onto my ass. When I laid on the ground and glared at the sky, I picked up a leaf and looked at the blood that coated it, smiling.

Is it time for me to go home now? Can this shit end? When will it end?

The blood looked like it was mixing with the shiny coating of it, no different than my blood sinking into the pores of my skin the longer I lay here. Holy shit.

Then the thought just hit me, my blood that's coating this leaf is like my skin, and the leaf is the underlying layer of my flesh. I am this leaf, and this leaf is me. I was told a long time ago by my teacher that all is one, and one is all.

I chuckled to myself as my vision started to fade, and I felt my heart slowing down like a machine waning, "I am this leaf, and this leaf is me, to the dirt I return," and my tears fell, "I love you," I finally said, and everything faded to black.

"HEY! GET YOUR ASS UP!" I heard Nessa's voice echoing in the darkness, but I feel light now, almost weightless like I'm floating. This feeling is nice. I don't feel pain. It's peaceful here.

I'm not sure how much time passed, but I remember waking up in someone's arms and voices I couldn't recognize shouting and cursing. Then another fiery pain jolted me from my unconscious, and when I looked down, Fox was cauterizing my wound after she had disinfected it.

I grabbed hold of someone's jeans and screamed when the flame torched my flesh. My tears fell, and my throat was hoarse from screaming in pain until I passed out again, hearing more voices in the darkness.

"Hey! Don't you fuckin die on me!" Fox shouted, "Son of a bitch!" I heard a dude's voice holler at me.

"I don't believe this shit," Another dude complained.

"It looks like she's not invincible," Another female said.

"WILL YOU SHUT THE FUCK UP, OR I WILL GUT YOU LIKE A PIG!" I heard another female voice argue. Oh, I think that's Nessa.

So who's the one holding me?

"You said we would all make it out of this shit alive, and that includes you!" Fox said, and I could tell she was trying to reach me while I was only half-conscious.

Then I passed out again.

When I woke up, I was lying in someone's lap and heard the sound of a roaring river nearby. Then the overwhelming smell of ointment and burning flesh wafted in my nose, and I tried not to hurl. God, I'm so fucking cold. Why is it so damn cold?

"Guys, she's freezing and sweating," I heard Nicks's voice shout, "Give her some blankets and make her drink some water," Nessa ordered.

"Why are we all worried about her anyway? Let her die since she seemed like she was happy to in the first place," I heard Derek say in the distance.

Then I saw Fox smack the shit out of him, hard enough, so he fell back.

"You ungrateful little bitch! She damn near died trying to protect your spoiled ass, and you got the fucking nerve to tell me she should've died. Maybe you should've died instead since you're useless to this entire group and me! Same to you, Jasmine. All I've heard you do is complain, bitch, whine and moan. I'm shocked that even after everything you've seen, you STILL don't fucking get it. Do me a favor and get the fuck outta my sight, or I WILL shoot you in the fucking knees, and you better pray I miss otherwise, you're gonna be limping the entire way out of this, and don't you dare ask any of us to carry you cuz I got no problem leaving your sorry asses behind!" She shouted.

I think I saw Derek's eyes well with tears, and Fox hit Jasmine too until she flew back and landed on her ass. "Get the fuck outta my sight, both of you!" She said, grabbing the gun and aiming it at both of them, "You got three seconds!"

"Oh my God, okay!" Derek shouted, "ONE!" Fox said and fired a bullet past Jasmine to jolt her out of her daze, "Oh my fucking God, I'm going!" She cried.

"TWO!" And fired another bullet past Derek, "This bitch is insane!" He said, running towards the woods, out of our sight.

Nick then laid me on the ground, wrapped some blankets around, and gave me some water. As soon as the liquid hit my tongue, I drank all of it, and he held me in his arms to warm me up since we're so close to the river, it only makes things colder.

He lifted me and decided to sit closer to the fire, "Let go of me," I said wearily.

"No," was all he said in return as he sat down and tucked me into his core to give me some more warmth by laying my back against his chest.

"Dude, stop," I complained, "Shut the fuck up," he fussed, wrapping his arms around mine. He's so warm, not like the hardened toxic men I'm used to that are nowhere near as nurturing as he is now.

Then I fell back asleep, I really have no idea how long I was out for, but I woke up in the middle of the night, feeling light-headed.

Since I feel better, now is the time to have another meeting with everyone, but when I tried to stand up, I heard footsteps thunder towards me, and he yanked my wrist, "Go back to bed," Nick ordered.

"No, I have to tell everyone what our next move is, and I need to do it while I'm feeling a little better. I don't know how long I have," and then I started to cough hard enough for my lungs to burn, and my stomach gnawed at my insides.

"Well, listen, when we came back for you, we ended up cooking the bear you took down, so please sit down. I'll get everyone to come to you and get you some dinner,"

"Why are you being so nice to me all of a sudden? Don't tell me it's cuz we fucked one time, and now all of a sudden you trust me?" I challenged, then coughed until my throat started burning from the dryness of it.

He handed me a water bottle, and I popped the cap and drank all of it, trying to ignore the way my insides throbbed from drinking it. Goddamn they must have done a number on me if I can't drink fucking water. Well, at least the pain is a reminder my ass is alive, but barely.

I'm exhausted, my muscles feel like lead on my bones, I'm still fucking freezing, and I'm sweating like a goddamn pig, it hurts to breathe, but it's because I'm not recovered I have to tell someone what our next move is, in case I still die in this shit. Now that I know I'm incapacitated, I'm only going to slow the team down no different than Jasmine and Derek in this situation, so I'm gonna advise they leave me behind.

I can already think of who's not gonna like it, but this is what's best for the group and not just myself.

My hands started to shake, and I grit my teeth to try and stop myself from trembling cuz of my exhaustion. I probably look pale as all hell right now, but this is the price of being the leader.

"What is it?" Derek snapped as all of them sat around me one after another until we were in a circle in front of the fire.

I coughed as blood and mucus-filled my palm, goddammit.

"Listen to me, here's what's gonna happen; Kim and Georgia are more than likely in one of the cabins watching us like a hawk, and since she's out of resources, she's gonna be cornered—" and coughed some more until I started to shake. The group fell silent.

"Dude, you're really dying?" Derek said with worry in his voice, "Yes, it's the other reason I'm gonna tell all of you to leave me behind," I said, not realizing blood was dripping down to my chin. I didn't feel the need to hide my exhaustion.

"In case I'm wrong, and one of them comes after us, I'll be the one to fight them before I die. I made a promise—" and coughed so hard I started tearing up, "that I was gonna die fighting and not like a coward," I wheezed.

"No fucking way," Fox argued.

"I will not leave you behind," Nessa fussed.

"Why are you so adamant about dying anyway?" Nick asked me, "For the same reason, I'm adamant about all of you making it out alive," I explained.

"But why do you always have to be the one to sacrifice yourself for us! Haven't you done enough! Haven't you died enough!?" Fox rebutted.

"Hey, Tessa," Derek finally called to me, "Yeah?"

"How much pain are you really in? And don't lie to me," He said.

"My muscles feel like lead, I'm light-headed and dizzy, it hurts to breathe, I'm losing water by sweating, and I'm fucking freezing. My lungs and throat are on fire, and it's why I'm not asking—I'm telling you to leave me behind," I said, meeting Derek's gaze.

"You do look like hell, but it's the first time I feel like you're telling me the truth," He admitted.

"Then leave me behind in case Georgia comes after us. Find the cabin Kim is staying in, and Nessa torture her until she confesses. I know that's something you can do," I shivered under the blanket.

She nodded her head and said nothing in return. It's her way of honoring me as my final wishes, "I need her to confess and tell the truth even if it's so you guys can hear it from her mouth and not to take my word for it,"

"I still don't get it. Why would you even be willing to go that far for us? Especially when Fox is right, all I have been doing is bitching the entire time," Jasmine said, glaring at me with concern.

"I don't—" then coughed till my lungs and throat burned, "like repeating myself, but I'll repeat it," and took a sip of water from the bottle beside me, "it's because of the life I lived before coming here, I don't want any more innocent people to die like this. I want you all to live your lives as normal people and not like me," then spat more blood and mucus into the ground, "I'm asking you to live normal lives, and it makes me selfish, I know, but it's the reason I stayed behind."

Then silence fell over us all.

"You did save my life now that I think about it,"

"And you were the first one to bandage my wound when I got shot the first time," Jasmine admitted.

"This is what I'm asking you to do; make sure to pack all of our supplies, leave me with a few weapons so I can defend myself if need be while you guys look for Kim. We head out in the morning,"

"Fuck that! We're taking a rest day," Nick snapped, grabbing some cooked bear meat over the open fire and handed it to me, "I'm not letting you die in this shit pit,"

"We've been through too much shit for me to just leave you here. What kinda sister would I be if I just left you here and I ran like a little bitch?" Fox added.

"I will honor whatever you wish," Nessa agreed.

"As much as I don't wanna admit it, I actually agree with them, you're more vital to our team than I care to admit, and honestly, I could use the rest and sleep,"

"Our attackers don't care about that," I tried to say sternly, but I coughed at the end of it.

"But still, after everything that has happened, I wouldn't want it to go down like this," Jasmine chimed.

"Then we'll see how I feel after a day of rest since I'm outvoted, take shifts, and guard our stuff, dismissed," I said.

They didn't argue with me, just sat up and laid in their respective blanketed areas around the fire.

I decided to do what I could to scarf down the bear meat to stop my stomach from growling, then laid down next to Nick while he held me until I fell asleep again.

Tessa Parker

Needless to say, I slept for a day and a half and have no idea what took place while I was out, but I do know when I got up, Nick was by my side the entire time which is weird for me. But instead of fighting him, I decided to just let him and ask questions if I felt better later.

After I gathered myself making my own bathroom in the woods, I decided now would be a good time to try and clean myself and my wounds, "Here, I'll help," Nick offered when I tried to take my shirt off but struggled cuz of the pain in my wounds.

"I'm fine, I can—" and I winced in pain, "do it myself," I argued, then pain jolted up my spine until my arm went limp. Goddammit, this sucks so much ass.

"Told you," He teased, reaching for the bottom of my shirt and pulled it over my head, inspecting my wounds, until I was fully naked in front of him, but I'm not embarrassed about my body like everyone else around me is.

"How bad is it?" I asked, "It's not sexy I can tell you that much," he joked, rinsing his hands in the water, washing his hands with the bottle of milk and honey soap, then started to unwrap the bandages from my wound. Shit, the running water from the river is making me shiver so hard my teeth were chattering.

"I know it's cold, but we gotta disinfect it and put more ointment on it,"

"I know, I would do it myself if my arms weren't being a fuckin asshole," I griped, mad at my body for being a weak bitch.

Then I felt a sharp sting from the wound on the side, "Mm, mother fucker," I silently cursed under my breath, "Damn, you don't even holler when you're in pain, do you?"

"I try not to cuz I know if I do, I'll tip off the enemy of my location, so I'm used to it," I grimaced when his hands were running over my throbbing wound. I looked down, and yup, it is fucking gross looking; it's all inflamed, bruised, and filled with throbbing pus. Ew fucking gross.

"You weren't kidding about the unsexy part," I tried to joke through grit teeth the more his hands ran over my wound with the lathered soap, "Yeah, no, I really wasn't, but damn did they have it out for you,"

"Shocker," I said, trying not to laugh cuz it still hurts to breathe, "You feeling pain anywhere else?" He said, rinsing the soap from the wound in my side and moved on to lathering for the second injury in my shoulder, which also hurts like a bitch.

"Aside from being cold as hell, hurting to breathe, and the pain the soap and ointment is causing me, 'I'm peachy,"

"Hell of a way to die if you ask me," He laughed, "You're an asshole,"

"I know it's what girls like the most about me," he smiled, but it wasn't cocky like I'm used to from other men; it was calm with confidence behind it.

What the fuck is this between us? And why does he make me feel all warm and fuzzy? Ew, gross, stop it. He can still die at any moment, so stop—And he ran his hands over my body with the soap he had lathered in his palms to wash me since I couldn't do it myself, getting attached to him.

"Did you fall for me yet?" He commented when he lifted my breast and rubbed the soap under it, "You're lucky my arms don't work otherwise, I'd hit you," I glared at him.

"I know, that's why I said it," He replied with an almost boyish grin that shouldn't belong to a man that has stubble on his jaw like he does. Still, his eyes are nowhere near as dark as mine, and it makes me want to protect him in this shit, that much I can't lie to myself anymore.

He's been the only one really taking care of me, and it's weird to me. It didn't matter how often I tried to push him away; he was just as stubborn as me. We only fucked once, so why is he so adamant about wanting to take care of me?

It didn't help that the feel of his hands over various parts of my body made me hot and bothered, but I guess the blood flow is a good sign that I can make it out of this alive since now I'm not as cold anymore.

He grabbed some water from the river in a tiny bucket and dumped it on me. Now I'm cold again. "Ooo, you son of a bitch," I said, trembling.

"I know, almost done," He replied as he dried me off with a towel (thank you, Nessa and Fox, for packing all the shit we need) and delicately put ointment over my wounds.

I had to ask since it was starting to bother me, and sure it hurts to talk, but I don't care right now.

"Nick,"

"Sup?" He said, looking down since he's taller.

"Why are you taking care of me? It's not cuz we fucked once, is it? Or am I missing something? Like, what do you want from me?" I needed to know cuz it was nagging me to no end.

This can't be a thing, we could die at any moment, and even if we get out alive, there's no guarantee we'll end up together or anything, not that I would be totally averse to it, but there's no point. I don't want any more people dying because of me.

He smiled, "Nothing, I just know another strong person when I meet one, and honestly, like you, I care for you cuz I understand more than you think I do," he paused and reached for the kit to bandage my wound, "So when this shit is over, if I never see you again, I can walk away saying that I did my part in caring for a woman who took two bullets and almost got mauled by a bear for my ass to getaway. If that's not grounds for respect, admiration, and some type of care from me, I don't know what else is," he answered honestly like it was easy as breathing.

"Are you always this open with your feelings?"

"Nah, not really, but since your an honest person, it makes it easier for me to open up to you cuz forreal despite you thinking you thinking you're secretive, I understand you a lot based off of the little bit you did tell me about you," He admitted tying the bandage around my waist and moved onto my shoulder to bandage it.

"Really? What's that?" I scoffed, then ended up coughing more mucus and specks of blood on the dirt ground since I couldn't lift my hands to cover my mouth.

Nick grabbed a towel and placed it over my mouth for me to cough into it as he stepped in front to try and shield me from the rest of the group so they wouldn't keep seeing me in my weakened state. I damn sure appreciated it at the moment cuz I hate feeling this powerless. Fucking hate it.

"You're stubborn, prideful, always think you have to sacrifice yourself as the leader to save others, are willing to die for what you believe in, and as much as you hate to admit it, you hate being alone and genuinely do care about us and our survival even if we don't fully trust you. Trust me, I know this isn't the first time you've thrown yourself in the fire for someone else's survival. Your scars when we fucked told me all of that," He whispered, "And how do you figure all of that?" I dejected and coughed some more into the towel.

Fuck, my lungs are burning, "the way we fucked told me the truth about you, the way you looked at me, and the way you smiled in ecstasy. Forreal you were the only woman able to satisfy me that way, and I'm a horny bastard, but after we fucked I was good and have been for a minute, but that's not to say I don't wanna fuck you more. I meant it when I said we have to make it out of this shit alive so we can have a helluva lot more sex," he whispered in my ear. Now the blood is rushing, and I'm hot again, this shit feels like a fucking hot flash, and I'm so over it.

"Pervert,"

"Like you're not," He joked, pulling the towel away from my mouth and helped me get dressed.

"How did you know?" I teased.

He smirked, "I'm very perceptive when it comes to women, and that's why I also want you to know you're not real good at hiding your face," he laughed.

Nick laid me into the dirt on my backside and helped me into my pants since I still couldn't move my arms, then my shirt. Man, this sucks. I can't touch him right now cuz even though he's broad in shoulder width, kinda plump-ish with no muscle definition, and is comfy as hell to lay on, he's still sexy to me, and I'm low key kinda mad my arms aren't working. Ok, he's not like round or anything; he's actually got the frame to hold muscle, just doesn't have any and has fat that looks like muscle when it's not if that makes any sense?

"You hungry? Are your arms still not working?"

"Nope, still not working, and now I'm worried," I replied, trying not to show him that I'm actually terrified at what's happening with my body. He lifted me from the ground and walked me back to our respective bed laid out before the fire. I noticed how Ness and Fox were smiling at Nick taking care of me, great now I'm gonna get made fun of for this shit.

"Well, first off, it's cool, don't panic. I know it hurts to breathe but try and stay calm, okay? Imma get you something to eat," He whispered in my ear.

"Hey, Nick! Why are you taking care of the Princess? I thought she could do it for herself since she's all big and bad," Derek teased, I think?

"Derek, I will shove my foot up your ass if you don't shut the fuck up," I argued, "Oo, someone's a little snappy," he laughed. Oh, he was teasing me.

"Of course she gets all the attention,"

"Well, last I checked, JASMINE, I took TWO bullets and almost got mauled by a bear. Thank you!" I replied, trying not to laugh since it feels like we're finally bonding now.

"And I got shot twice! So fuck you, Tessa," Derek rebutted.

"Uh yeah, I got shot once too!" Jasmine reminded.

I laughed, and then I started coughing again but couldn't cover my mouth, but before my cough became violent, Nessa ran to me with a towel in hand and wiped my mouth, saying nothing.

"How bad is it?" She asked me in Russian, "bad, everything hurts,"

"At least your alive," She joked, "barely," I tried not to laugh, but it made Nessa smile. We both have fucked up humor like that.

"Whatchu guys talking about?"

"We're joking about how she's dying," Nessa explained plainly.

"You guys are so fucked up," Jasmine said, "you guys have fucked up humor,"

"People die in my country all the time, so it's something I can joke about. It's why we are as tough as we are,"

"And nurturing, don't forget," I told her in Russian, "And yes, nurturing cuz we know how fleeting life is," she replied in her language with a warm smile.

"Rest more, I stand guard," Nessa said, "Kay," I replied.

So I laid there, helpless and at the mercy of Nick and Fox at the moment. It looks like my hunch was correct; no one has been after us, which tells me that they are in the cabin nearby and are waiting for us to strike them, but I'm only holding up the team, and the enemy can strike at any time. Dammit, I have got to get better sooner, and now is the time for me to start praying.

Chapter 4: The Leaders Past
Kalina (Fox) Izumi

It was good to see someone taking care of her, especially since I finally got over my own shit, but not gonna lie; Kim almost fooled me. I stared at her sleeping frame, and my heart sank at how pale she looked in the face; she really did take those bullets for us so we could get out alive.

What kinda person is she to do something like that? Cuz, let's be honest, I've only known this girl for what? A couple of months if that, and she lays her life on the line like that? For my spoiled, ungrateful ass, and it's why Jasmine and Derek are getting on my fucking nerves.

They have no idea the kinda person she is, and sure I was pissed with her for using me as bait for us to get out, but when I think back on it, she only did what was necessary to get us all out alive. As fucked up as it is, she makes the hard decisions none of us are strong enough to make, not even Nessa as much as a hard-ass as she comes off.

She's been reticent lately except for when we hang out at night away from everyone, its the only time I've heard her talk about a future with her husband, even though she seems so far removed from everything. It makes me wonder what the fuck happened to them that makes both Tess and Nessa so damn removed from everything? But still able to care?

"You worried about her?" Derek asked with a biodegradable plate of bear meat, and I shot him a glare, "Yeah, I am," I admitted.

"She's such a bitch, though," Jasmine complained, tossing a stick into the river and watched it go down, "I know she is. Hell, she used me as bait to get us all out alive the first time we were in the woods. But the truth is, she makes the hard decisions none of us can make," I mentioned honestly.

They glared at me dumbfounded, and I decided now would be a good time to explain what happened in detail and why I believe her and her gift.

It's funny. This is probably the one time I'm hoping her gift is the reason she comes back alive, though my gut is telling me if she doesn't make it out, she will die this time.

Hell how many times did she die for our mistakes? I couldn't think about it cuz all it would do is make me angry at myself, somehow knowing she has to carry all that shit alone.

"She did all of that? How the hell did she know how they were gonna move?" Nick asked while rubbing her hair to comfort her since she was shivering in her sleep. It made me smile at the sight of it; she needs a reason to live, hell we all do.

"Because she thinks like them, she thinks like a hunter would," Nessa answered before I had a chance to say the exact same thing.

I can say it's nice that the three of us are a unit finally where we don't have doubts or hesitation. I realize now everything Red said to me in the van back then was the truth about us, and even human beings in general.

It's still not gonna stop me from trying to be normal, but it won't be without accepting this part of myself regardless of how long it takes. Even if it hurts to do that, I will, at all costs, for my family. I never want them to see this side of me, ever.

Tess is right. I'm not a civilian anymore. The longer I stare at her wounded and barely breathing reminds me of that. So for once, I'm asking to carry my own weight in this shit and not be someone that holds the team back anymore.

"Do you guys even really know about her or her past? Has she told any of you that?" Jasmine asked out of curiosity, and I shook my head no, "She hasn't divulged that to me," I replied, staring to the other side of the river where more trees lined beside it.

"Fox, as much as I hate to say it, I know why but I cannot tell you why as it would mean all of us would die if we knew the truth about her past," Nessa warned, and it made my stomach clench. When the hell did she tell Nessa and not me?

"Think of all the stuff you've seen in urban movies and why she would know all of those languages to begin with. That's the only hint I'm allowed to give you without telling you," Nessa said, knowing I was confused and wanted to know. Hell, I deserved to know.

Urban films? Do you mean like drugs and stuff?

"What languages did you say she speaks again?" I asked Nessa, and she smiled warmly where she sat a little further from me closest to the river, "Russian, Spanish, Portuguese, and Arabic,"

"I don't get it," Derek chimed.

Wait a minute, urban films, and those languages—

My eyes bulged from my sockets, and I stared harder at Nessa, "no fucking way," I said, somehow trying not to be over-emotional, but when it hit me, it was hard not to be upset at the truth of her past.

That's why she used the word comrade and not friends. Oh my God.

"Wait a second, you're not telling me she used to do THAT kind of work? Are you?"

"It's why she had to change her name and come here to our school," Nessa said as if she knew the truth, "Trust me, I was upset when I found out too, but you have to promise never to spill the truth."

"What the fuck are you guys talking about now?!" Jasmine demanded to know, and when I looked over at Nick, he paled, "No wonder she kicked my ass when we fought. Fuck me, dude, she's way more dangerous than all of us combined," he answered my own suspicions.

Nessa nodded her head, "so if any of you are smart, you would listen to her, and it's why I am and trust her need to redeem herself for that type of work she used to do in her past she will never say to any of us," She replied.

"You've got to be fucking kidding me," I shook my head in disbelief.

There's no way to have a gift like that and to STILL kill other people? How many times has she stepped over dead bodies and corpses as far as the eye can see? How many times did she die in her visions or almost died in real life?

"Please no, don't leave me, please," I heard her tremble a whisper and noticed she was crying in her sleep, and not gonna lie, it broke something inside of me to see it.

Goddammit.

"EXCUSE ME!? Are any of you gonna clue us in!?" Jasmine said, throwing another stick at Nessa, but she ignored it and her altogether.

"I've said all I can," Nessa replied to them both and returned her sights to the water, lost in her own thoughts.

"Wow, urban films and multiple languages, what's so impressive about that?" Derek said, still confused, and I shook my head, "Guys, you really don't understand. Tess is DANGEROUS, hell even more dangerous than Kim, and it's why she had no problem staying behind and took not one bullet, but two and damn near got mauled by a fucking bear. She is NOT to be fucked with," I tried to explain with urgency.

It was hard for me not to be scared of her, but then when I think about her smile and the few times she hugged me feverishly when we made it out, she apologized for what she made me do and specifically said, "I will carry the weight like I always do, and for that I'm sorry."

The truth hurt more than believing she was just another college student like us, and it made me want to scream, shout, kick and punch something simultaneously.

"How long did she say she did that for?"

"Think on what she has said to either of us," Nessa said only to me, "She did say she doesn't want to see any more people die and that she never wanted to go back to that life like she did when she was—" Nick was saying, filling in the blanks with us at the same time.

"A teenager," he finally uttered, "No fucking way," I said with shock and rage in my voice.

"Why the hell are you so upset about it anyway? Whatever IT is," Jasmine commented.

"I'm not mad that she lied to me, or us all, but what I'm upset about is knowing she's been carrying this shit alone her entire life, and now it makes sense why she would be so willing to sacrifice herself to get all of us out. It still makes ME feel useless compared to her," I admitted more to myself out loud than anyone else.

Son of a bitch, Tess.

I want to hate her, but I can't.

"I may be from the streets, but I can do something to protect her and not be a fuckin pussy about all of it and this entire situation,"

"Well fuck you, I still want to go home and forget all of this shit happened, to begin with. I still don't believe that Kim killed her mother, let alone everything else," Jasmine argued.

"Then go eat her pussy while you're at it hoe. I'm so over your bitching," I snapped.

Nick laughed, and I heard Nessa chuckle.

"The fuck did you say to me?!" Jasmine challenged me, "Fighting me would not be a good idea," I warned.

I'm not the same person I was when this trip started.

"Well, why don't you suck on Tess's clit while you're at it," Jasmine rebutted.

"That's not an image I need in my head right now," Nick commented, "Will you please SHUT UP!" Derek mentioned to Nick.

"Trust me, if she ever swung that way, I would,"

"I need both of you to fuck me when we make it out of this alive, thanks," Nick said out of nowhere, and I couldn't help but laugh at him by how open and honest he was, not like the guys I used to flirt with for the hell of it cuz not gonna lie I've always loved the attention. Which only made his honesty even more hilarious to me.

"Sure, dude, that's only if Tess doesn't die on us,"

"Bet," He agreed with a boyish grin on his lips, and now I can see why Tess likes him so much. I never thought I would go for an honest man like him, cuz truthfully I prefer a guy to butter me up with flowers, dinner, and stuff, but I've always been curious to have a one-night stand.

"Ew, you guys are gross. I would fuck just about ANYONE than either of you," Derek fake gagged.

"Ouch, way to be a dick," I laughed at him.

"I'm not, I'm jus saying, none of you are my type,"

"Let me guess, tall beefy white guys are your type,"

"Oh fuck off, Fox," He fussed.

I shot him a blank stare, "I would never fuck you even if we were the last two people on earth."

"DAAAAAAAMN!" Nick jeered.

Then I heard Nessa laugh at us, and it was good to know she does laugh and smile sometimes, which made me feel better about this entire shitty situation.

"Will all of you please SHUT UP about fucking, JEEZ!"

"Aint shit else to do while we're waiting for Tess to recover since I'm not leaving her behind,"

"Still, Tess is bae, so I ain't doing shit without her permission, cuz she's mine," He claimed.

"Ooo, someone's sprung," I joked with him. No wonder Tess likes him so much.

"Listen, I've never found someone I vibe with, and I've been with a LOT of bitches. It's that simple for me, and I don't bother trying to complicate things. My life back at home is already fucked up enough,"

"Well, I say while we wait, let's have storytime! Nessa, you first,"

"I'll pass," She immediately rejected.

"Well, there isn't much to say about me; I come from a middle-class family, both Japanese and Black. My mom is black, and my dad is Japanese, and I gotta tell you it makes for a funny ass dynamic, I have a little sister who I love more than anything in this world, and she's who I'm trying to make it back to out of this shit. My major is Engineering, and my minor is Journalism. What about you guys?" I asked, deciding to be the first to admit a little about myself.

"I have no family and only have my husband. I've been hardened by growing up in Moscow alone and one day wish to have a family with my husband should he make it out of the military alive. So he is who I wish to make it back to. My major is Nursing with a minor in Dance," Nessa finally admitted a little more about herself, and it made me wonder why she grew up alone? Is that why she and Tess get along so well?

"Aint shit for me to tell, I grew up in the streets of Chicago and have my ma and two baby sisters I need to make it back to cuz my dad is a piece of shit who left us to go live with some other bitch in another state. My major is Computer Science with no minor, okay Jasmine, your turn," He passed the buck around, and it made me smile to know something about him, and now I really see why Tess likes him as much as she does.

"Ugh, do I have to?" She whined, and I tossed a stick at her, "Yes, you do."

"UGH, FINE! Jasmine, I come from a rich family, so I don't got any long sob story to tell,"

"That's not what Tess told me, so now I know you're lying,"

"The fuck does that mean? What did she tell you about me?"

"Jasmine, yet again, out of her spoiled attitude, thinks she deserves to know.

"All you care about is being seen with Kim cuz you wanna be pretty, and popular and not a wannabe and are easily swayed by the crowd cuz at the end of the day you refuse to face the truth that you're not wanted by someone in your family, and it's why you STILL want Kim to accept you as badly as you do. I took psychology, FYI, and it's why I know you're full of shit," I called out.

Everyone got silent, and Jasmine stomped to me and tried to punch me, but I blocked it and shoved her on her ass, "What the fuck would you know about it anyways! You all come from a family that loves you! So fuck you for thinking you guys know anything when none of you KNOW SHIT about me! UGH, I HATE ALL OF YOU!" She shouted, then stormed off into the woods to stop herself from crying.

"Damn, that was harsh," Nick mentioned, "Someone had to give this bitch a reality check and better me than anyone else cuz no one else will tell her. It's the other reason she's still stuck on pretty and refuses to accept what's happening, even now,"

"Cut the girl some slack. None of us are LIKE YOU," Derek defended.

"Fuck you, Derek, you think I didn't start out like you! In fact, I DID start out like you, the entire time I was the one whining, crying, and complaining the first time we got lost in these fucking woods, targeted by people who wanted nothing more than to see my ass DEAD, so yeah I know what the fuck I'm talking about," I fussed, "Not to mention I was almost RAPED in those fucking woods, so none of you can tell me shit," I finished.

Then I noticed Derek's sad smile, "Yeah?"

"Yeah, Derek, that's what happened. I slit the dude's throat and heard him beg me not to, I still have fucking nightmares cuz it was my classmate in Philosophy. You think that shit don't haunt me like none of this shit don't haunt me. Fuck you for thinking it don't," I ended.

Silence fell over us for a second.

"You said he's dead, right?" Nick said in a low growl, "Yeah, he's dead, and I'm the one who killed him." I confessed.

Derek stared at me, stunned at my confession, "so you never really got over it did you?"

"No, and I never will," I replied.

"Fine then, my name is Derek; I'm bi-sexual, and when I came out to my parents, let's just say they don't accept me for who I am, and I've been trying to get out of that house since then. My major is Business with no minor. I can't say why I wanna live or that I have any one specific to make it back to cuz I don't have anyone to, other than just wanting to find someone to love me for me," He answered.

"That's cool, and hey, you'll get out of there someday and find someone who digs you for you," I tried to cheer him up.

His glare fell to a solemn expression, "I damn sure hope so, cuz I'm tired of being locked in that goddamn wooden box whenever I try to talk to anyone I'm interested in, I get no privacy, and it's like being shackled," he slipped then clenched his jaw.

"Hey, I'm sorry you've gone through that. Hell, I'm sorry we've all been through some shit. But it's why we need to make it out of this alive," I reminded.

"I guess I should look at this fucked up situation as a blessing in disguise, right?"

"Sure, why not?"

"Nevermind the fact I've seen my classmates killed and plucked off like flies, and I'm gonna have nightmares for the rest of my life," He joked, finally.

"Hey Nessa, can I ask you a question," Derek said to her, "Yes?"

"You said you grew up alone? Why is that? I mean, it's cool if you don't wanna share, you peg me as a really private person."

"Since we are comrades, it is because my family was brutally murdered in front of me as a child and why I never want to be that weak again. My husband is the one who trained me in combat and weapons. But it why I wish to be a nurse instead to heal others instead of consistent killing to survive in this world," she said casually. Like it caused her no type of pain at all, mentioning it.

How the hell do she and Tess do that?

"How can you say you love him then if he did all of that to you?!" Derek said, shocked at her confession. Hell, I was too.

"It is out of love and my desire to be strong he did when he did not have to," She explained, and now I think I admire her more than I did before this whole thing started. That's why she and Tess got along so well.

Then we all fell silent for a moment, "Guys, we're gonna make it out of this alive. So Derek can find love, so Nick and I can make it back to our families. And so Nessa can have a family with the man she loves. All of those dreams are worth it, and I think Tess knows that about each of us and the other reason why she, like Nessa and me, fight as hard as we do for all of you. So this time, I'm asking all of you to put all of that shit aside and help us as a team do what's needed for us to live," I pleaded one more time.

"You got it," Nick agreed.

"I got no other choice, do I?" He commented, moving the tendrils of his long brown hair from his eyes to look at me with a sardonic smile, "Nah, you really don't."

"Come on, Nessa, teach us all how to shoot and to fight so we don't slow the group up," I said, and she nodded her head standing up, and grabbed her gun to teach us how to survive in this shit.

We have to make it out alive.

Chapter 5: Denial
Tessa (Red) Parker

When I woke up, I definitely felt better and noticed everyone was talking to each other, except I couldn't find Jasmine. Where the hell did she go? I thought, sitting upright from the ground, grabbed the gun beside me and asked, "Where is Jasmine?"

"She's off in the woods somewhere," Derek explained, "I'm gonna go get her. I don't need someone targeting her in case Georgia decides to move on us,"

"Whats make you so sure she would?"

"Because Georgia trusts Kim with her life and would do anything she says because of their bond, and it's why I have to be the one to defend Jasmine," I explained.

They all glared at me with a weird sense of admiration, and it was strange. What the hell happened when I was knocked out?

"I'll go with you," Nick volunteered to take another gun on the ground, loaded it, and walked behind me, saying nothing.

"Be careful," Fox called out.

I nodded and walked further into the forest, and since it was dark out, I did what I could to adjust my vision to find her.

When I finally saw her, she was sobbing under the tree, muttering how much she hates this shit. What the hell happened when I was asleep?

"Nick, cover me," I ordered when I walked closer to her, "Don't you take another fucking step! I hate all of you cuz you're all fucked up and insane. Not me!" She croaked.

So I kept a respectable distance and knelt to her, "Hey, what the hell happened? I'm here if you need to talk, and listen; I'm sorry I've been so hard on you," I admitted sincerely.

"Fuck you! None of you understand me! Or how traumatizing this whole thing has been for me!" She sobbed, "I'm not like any of you, I don't have some traumatic fucked up story to share. I'm normal, not any of you. All of you have fucked up lives, and I DON'T!"

"Sounds like denial," Nick called out, "Shut up, Nick!" I defended.

"Leave me the hell alone so I can just die,"

"Not gonna happen,"

"So then what? You'll drag me out of here like you did when you knocked me out! What the fuck is wrong with you!? Can't you take a fucking message!" She kept fighting me.

"Jasmine, who do you wanna make it back to?"

"No one, I just want things to go back to the way they were when I was waking up with my servants dressing me! Where my breakfast was made for me every day! I want my limo back, I want my nice clothes, I'm tired, everything stinks, I'm dirty all the goddamn time! I want my room back, I want to be normal again!" And I knew she was cracking under pressure. I know the feeling.

I sat down in front of her, "Jasmine, I'm sorry this all happened, but I need you to put all of that aside if you can so you can make it back to that life, and you can forget all of this even happened, please?" I asked.

"Fuck you, I can't. I'm not strong like any of you. I can't do this shit, I can't stop playing in my head seeing Courtney fall to the ground like that, I can't stop playing the screams in my head. This shit is so fucked up! I don't wanna be here anymore. I want to go the fuck home!" She sobbed, pulling her knees to her chest and buried her face away from me.

"Jasmine, I need you to be strong."

"I can't," she cried.

I sighed, put my weapon down, and laid on the ground, deciding to stare at the sky to not take such a threatening stance to her letting silence fall over us to where all I could hear were her choked sobs.

"I didn't come from a rich family, so I don't know what that's like, and I won't lie and say I understand, but I definitely relate to wanting things to go back to the way they were," I admitted.

"What the fuck would you know about it! You don't know a damn thing," She snapped.

I smiled sardonically, counting the stars, "I lost count of how many people have died in front of me and how many people I've done the same in return. I've been running from my past for a long time Jasmine, and it's why I can't run anymore. I'm tired. So just like you, all I wanted was to be normal, but when I was lying here dying, I grabbed a leaf and looked at the way it was covered with my blood; it reminded me that my life meant something and that I was able to be useful to someone. I still don't give a shit about dying. I've seen it and felt it so many damn times; I'm numb to it," I said.

"So what? That doesn't mean anything to me," She replied in between, crying.

"I've lost so many friends, family, one after another, and it's why I can never be normal and why my life is cursed with whoever gets close to me. I have no reason to live cuz everyone I've ever loved is dead. You have a life worth going back to, Jasmine; you have people who love you who I'm sure you haven't thought about. Tell me one person."

"No, no one loves me. It's why I don't want to fight anymore. I'm tired and just want to end it here," She cried.

"What about your family?"

"No, they're always gone leaving me behind cuz all they care about is money and not me," she told me honestly.

I counted 23 stars at this point and kept going, "what about a love interest? Do you believe in love?" I asked.

"No, everyone who's ever gotten close to me only wants to use me for my money, and it's why Kim is the only one I trusted, I just wanted to be seen with her so I could have more money, status, and power. And it's why I hate Fox and you for being so honest and strong,"

"You have any siblings?" I asked, "No. Just me,"

"What about a friend?" I said, and she finally went silent, "No, she's always busy with her own life and doesn't care about me like I care about her."

"Romantically, I'm assuming?" I called, and I heard more leaves rustle, and she cried harder, "I've been in love with her for a long time, and I can never tell her, it's why I'm so alone, and I just wanna die here, I fucking quit,"

"So you don't wanna live to tell her one day how you feel?"

"What for when all she's gonna do is reject me?" She argued.

"I'll tell you a secret," I confessed and let my tears fall again silently, "My brother was raped in front of me to remind me that I have no protector and that I'm all I have in this world. Shortly afterward, he hung himself in his room we lived in," I confessed. I felt Nicks's eyes on me, and I knew he was mortified at what I had just admitted.

"I never told him that I forgave him and that it wasn't his fault for not being able to protect me," I kept counting more stars as more tears fell, "I never got to tell him I loved him, and I can never forget his screams of pain or the way he fought them as best as he could to protect me. So please," I pleaded with her, "I'm asking you to live so you can tell her how much you do love her,"

"I got a helluva lot of regrets in this life, Jasmine, so please, I'm asking you to fight for the desire to tell her how you feel. Even if she turns you down, this pain will pass despite how it feels," I reassured. She stopped crying and said nothing for a moment.

"Oh my God, I'm—I'm so sorry. I had no idea,"

"That's just one of many sins I carry, just like my only desire for all of us to make it out alive. I'm not a good person Jasmine, none of us are, but it's why I can't stop trying to save lives instead of taking it. So if I have to be the monster so someone else can live, then so be it," I replied, finally counting 32 stars in the sky.

"I'm so sorry. I really am a piece of shit, aren't I?"

"No, Jasmine, just a normal human being like all of us," I smiled sarcastically, trying to tune out his screams and the way he called out to me in his final moments of it.

"Fox wasn't lying when she said you do care? About all of us?" She asked, "No, she wasn't lying, and yes, I've been hard on you, and for that, I'm sorry. I'm just hardened by my shitty life," I replied.

I heard leaves rustle nearby, and without warning, I jolted to my feet, grabbed my gun, and stepped in front of Jasmine to shield her while Nick fired shots from his weapon, "We got company!" He shouted.

"Son of a bitch! I called it!" I argued.

"Jasmine, go back to camp now! Tell them Georgia is shooting at us and to get the fuck outta here now!" I ordered, "I can't. I'm scared."

"GO NOW!" I shouted, shoving her so she would get the message and run, "OW GODDAMMIT!" Nick hollered in pain. When I turned to look, he had been shot in the chest, and my heart fell out of my ass, no no, no, not another one, please God, not another one.

"Oh my God! Nick's been shot!" Jasmine called out and ran back to camp, "JASMINE, GET DEREK AND FOX HERE NOW! TELL NESSA TO LEAD THE REST OUT OF HERE!" I said, deciding to step over Nick and look for my target. I'm gonna murder this bitch with my own two hands.

Needless to say, I blacked out after seeing Nick lying there groaning in pain, cuz that was all it took for me to go back to that dark place inside of me.

The moments that passed faded in and out, I remember aiming the end of my gun at her, screaming, and blood. So much more blood. I fired more shots cuz when I finally came back from my reverie, I glared down at her corpse and saw the blood spurting from her chest and the way it pooled into the leaves and dirt. The way her empty brown-eyed glare of agony stared into the sky only adds to my nightmares of the shit I've seen in this life.

When I didn't hear any more shots fired, I knelt to her and closed her eyes, then prayed over her and myself. I needed it more than anyone cuz something tells me she caught the blunt end of my rage when she shot Nick.

Shit! Nick! I finished my prayer and darted back to the camp, but they were all gone, including Nick. Son of a bitch! Well, now I'm back in this shit alone, I just pray they made it out safely.

When I finally found them by following the trail of blood, my heart stopped at the sight of Nick slumped in Nessa's arms as she tried to treat the wound in his chest, "It missed his heart but barely," She said to me in Russian.

I let out a sigh of relief, but now it's my turn to take care of him, and the team cuz now is our time to move and end this shit for good.

Another night passed, and I spent that time taking care of Nick, and the rest of the team, making sure everyone was okay, especially Jasmine, "You good?" I asked.

"I guess so," was all she would say, but I'll take it for what it's worth for now.

To my surprise, Nicks got the fighting spirit of any man I've ever met and refused to give up and die in this place despite how both of our bodies are now fucked up. He still kept making jokes to not worry me, and all it did was aggravate me, fucker.

Needless to say, when everyone was fully healed up, we have now officially run out of resources and need to plan our attack on the cabin in the morning, so we can finally nail Kim, cuz if she's smart, she wouldn't be stupid enough to come after us. She's too bougie for that. Like Jasmine, I can rely on her sole need to be the one in charge to watch us all die in this mess.

"We leave tonight for our Cabins," I told them, "Cool, then what?" Derek asked.

"We make Kim talk and tell us the truth as far as what she has planned for the school, and why she killed her mother then we grab as much of our stuff and get the fuck outta here, assuming the bus is still here, but I'm not sure. Does anyone still have their cell phone so we can call for help once we make it back to the cabins?"

"I mean not really, cuz Kim took all of our phones before this whole 'game' started," Derek reminded me, "Got it, so more than likely she's holding all of our stuff in her cabin, and it's possible she set traps for us in the other cabins, so we have to be strategic about the whole thing,"

"But how the hell would we KNOW which one she's staying in?"

"There's probably some secret bunker in one of them,"

"Well, listen, there's me, Nick, Fox, Nessa, Derek, and Jasmine. How many cabins were there when we got here?" I asked, seeing if any of them were paying attention, "Shit, like what? Six? I think?" Nick said.

"So then, how will we know for sure?" Fox asked me, "Its also a possibility that she has more than one that has a bunker in it, so there's one person for every cabin, and we're running low on resources,"

"So then, how would any of us be able to let the other know we found the crib?" Nick said, "I haven't thought on that yet, but assuming there's wifi and if I had to safely assume computers in each bunker, Nick, you said you were in computer science, right?"

"Yep, sure did,"

"Anyway, you can hack a signal for help? That way, if one of us does find her, we at least know the cops would be on their way up here to get us out of this shit?"

"I don't know, but I can try,"

"What if one of us dies? How would we know?" Jasmine said with fear in her voice, "You want me to go with you?" I offered.

"Please? I'm too scared to fight on my own," She whispered, "It's cool, and listen, the best thing would be to have us meet in the centerfire pit at daybreak.

Whoever isn't here by then can safely assume they're dead and need to find a ride out of here,"

"That's so fucked up," Derek commented.

"It's the majority over the minority," I explained.

"No, I get it, it makes sense, but we still haven't figured out how to notify the other one if we found her? What then?" Derek said, and it made me happy to know he was invested in our plan, I wonder what happened to make him change his mind?

"I need to think on that one a little more," I said honestly to the group, "Any ideas?" I asked the team, and we all fell silent for a few moments thinking this over carefully.

"Does she have cameras at all?" Nick asked out of the blue, and Fox beamed, "Hell yeah, she does! I noticed a small one, but it was barely there in the living room, so who knows where she has them placed around in the house."

"So assuming she is watching all of us infiltrate the cabins in a bunker somewhere, is it possible to transmit the mainframe to the other monitors in other cabins so we can signal the other that one of us found her? Meet at a rendezvous location and go back together as a group?"

"Okay, that helps the notifying part, but what about timing? What if we're too far in, or one of us get snagged by some random ass trap like what you think it might be?" Fox commented.

"Then whoever can see the signal are the ones who meet up at said cabin as a group, then we regroup as to who isn't with us and do a rescue mission."

"What if one of us is the one that finds her, and we miss the signal?"

"Then it's safe to assume that's the one she's in, which would turn into a rescue mission instead," I affirmed.

"Damn, you really do think all of this shit out," Nick said with a smirk on his lips, "Get serious, will you?"

"I am. I'm jus saying its sexy,"

"Can we PLEASE just focus on the mission?" Derek whined.

I rolled my eyes and tried to fight a smile but returned to the topic at hand, "Don't assume anything, be on your toes, and remember, any and everything around you is a weapon. Do what you can to live and make it back. We meet in the morning, and whoever isn't with us, we're leaving behind. That includes me, understood?" I said sternly.

Nessa nodded her head, and the rest said nothing in return.

"I can't hear you. Is that understood?" I demanded, "yes," they all reluctantly admitted.

"This is gonna be an overnight mission, so we all need to get some sleep, drink the rest of the water, and scope out each cabin thoroughly, be careful of traps, and fight for your life. Dismissed," I said, sitting up from the group and walked away.

"Please, God, let me be right, and we all make it out alive, I can't lose any more people like this," and at the end of the day, I will make Kim tell the truth about what she did and her plans with the school.

Chapter 6: Conquer Your Fear
Tessa (Red) Parker

When nightfall came, we huddled together, "Guys, we got this, don't be scared, we've made it this far as a team, rely on your own strength, and regardless we have until dawn to make this mission a success. We're all in this together, and when we make it out alive, we will never speak of this to anyone ever and can go back to our normal lives. Promise?" I reassured with a warm smile on my lips.

"How are you so calm?" Jasmine finally asked me, "Cuz I'm not afraid to die and don't got shit else to lose anymore. You can't take from me what hasn't already been taken," I answered.

Again, Derek, Nick, and Fox looked at me with admiration, and Nessa just smiled, "Neither am I," Nessa replied.

"And it's why we're all gonna make it out of this shit alive," I said, opening my arms to them, "Come oooooon group hug!" I spoke with a wide smile.

"Ew, what are you like twelve?" Derek teased, "Shut the fuck up and give me a hug ass hat," I cursed, and each of them complied.

I relished in the warmth of them and vowed to myself if I could save any of them, I will, and even if one gets left behind, I plan to stay to protect them while the rest leave me behind if they have to. I care too much to let even one of us fall behind.

Then when we broke from our group hug, Nick kissed me out of nowhere, holding me to his lips by the back of my head, and goddamn, I would be lying if the feel of this man's lips on mine didn't make me insane. Ew, stop it. When he broke from my lips, he said nothing, winked, and returned to the rest of the group using the last bit of ammo we had to load his gun.

"Get a room, you two," Fox teased, and it was weird to see everyone smile, even Jasmine, which only melted my heart if I'm honest.

"You guys ready?" I said, "Not really," Derek complained.

"I'm ready to get some fuckin answers," Nick commented.

"I'm not," Jasmine admitted.

"You know I live for blood when it comes to people like Kim attacking innocent people," Nessa smiled with joy, "Let's end this shit for good," Fox said with firm gazes in my direction.

"Let's go," I ordered and walked ahead, following the markings we left on the trees back to the main cabins. When we made it back to the fire pit where this all started, I grit my teeth, trying not to growl at remembering how all this shit started to begin with. Nessa is like me; we personally can't stand people like Kim who attack civilians.

If you're gonna put up a fight, at least let it be someone like Nessa or me. It's no different than bullying someone weaker than you. It's fucking disgusting.

I put my hand in front and noticed all the lights were off in each Cabin, and the moonlight gave us just enough light for us to see the walkway up to each house. Good shit.

"Jasmine, stay with me, I want each of you to look for cell phones in each cabin if you can, and other weapons to keep on you, the more, the better, and Nick do what you can to get us the fuck outta here, I'm counting on you,"

"Got it, babe," and when he said babe, it made my heart leap to my throat. Oh my God, stop it.

"I'm going to the far left cabin," Nick said, "I got the center one next to Nicks house," Nessa chimed, "I got the one next to Nessa."

"I'll take the one next to Nessa and Derek; you take the one beside me to the right that way. If any of us are in trouble, we can easily get to the other one. Save the last one as a group, if there's any electricity do not turn the lights on and check the time on the oven or microwave if you can. Meet up in a few hours, which should be when the forest is the loudest if there's no clock. Now move out."

And one by one, they each walked cautiously to their respective cabins staying crouched. Who taught them that, I wonder? "Let's go, Jasmine," I said as she stood behind me while we crouched to our respective houses.

The doors were open in each of them, which tells me she's expecting us. Not a good sign. Shit, I forgot to mention what to do if there's flash or smoke bombs in case she's sneaky enough to use that kinda shit. Why didn't I think of that before? Goddammit.

"Stay low to the ground, and do not move unless I say so," I reminded, "Okay," she complied.

I walked through the hallway towards the living room, and thankfully the moonlight illuminated a tripwire in front of me and a few lasers in different places of the furnished living room. Son of a bitch.

"What's wrong?" Jasmine asked me, and I looked around to see if there were any weapons like guns or knife-like traps set in the walls or ceilings since the light from the moon was coming from the big window in the living room even though I was still in the hallway. Since I was trained to see in the dark, it makes this process easier. Yup, a minigun at the end of the hallway if I set off this tripwire, "Do not move," I warned.

"Why?" She asked, "Look down," I told her, and she did, "Oh my God is that what I think it is?" She said, "Now look above in the corner. Do you see that little black spot at the end of the hallway?"

She got real quiet for a second, "What is that?"

"That's a minigun that's going to shoot us if we set off any of these wires," I explained.

"But why?" she tried not to cry, "now do you believe me?" I asked her calmly, but she said nothing in return.

"Stay here. I'll scope the place out,"

"Wait! Don't leave me here,"

"I need you to leave if something happens to me to warn the others. Can you do that for me?" I said, turning to look back at her, and she looked horrified, "Why me?"

"Because I have to keep you safe, okay? I damn sure didn't go through all the shit I've been through in life not to make it count," I reminded.

She looked down at the rug-lined hallway by the entrance and shook her head, "Thank you."

I carefully stepped over the tripwire, making sure to keep my weight evenly distributed, and focused on my breathing as I moved further down the hallway.

When I made it to the end, I noticed lasers in various places in the living room, so I quickly scanned the area for other weapons around and found them in different corners of the room.

What about behind the walls? I had to assume there were fake walls in each cabin too.

Then I heard hollering from the following few cabins beside me. Shit.

"TESS, WHAT WAS THAT!" She shouted, and since she was loud, bullets started firing down, and my heart raced against my chest, "JASMINE RUN! NOW!" I ordered, but all I heard were her screams by the door, "Tess, I've been hit, I'm bleeding," GODDAMMIT!

Without thinking, I ran back to her, ignoring the last two bullets that ran through my leg and lower back since it didn't stop until I noticed she was crawling out the door towards the walkway, "I'm so tired of this shit!" Jasmine roared.

I buckled forward and grit my teeth when the blood ran down and stained my pants again, "you bitch I swear I'm gonna gut you like a fucking pig!" I growled with determination. Goddamn, this pain is a bitch and a half.

"Jasmine, get out of here now. I got this," I reminded, but she looked over her shoulder, mortified at the amount of blood I was losing, "What the hell happened?"

"I got shot twice, now get out of here!" I said, forcing myself to stand up and ignore the way my muscles twitched and slammed the door shut. Son of a bitch, I knew it was a bad idea to bring her with me, but this is what I get for wanting to play the hero.

She started banging on the door, "Tess! Don't leave me!"

"I'll come back for you, I promise," I lied. That last bullet is making it hard for me to stand, let alone crawl right now. But I can't give up. As much as I want to, I can't. I don't have much time to get this shit done and over with before I lose too much blood.

"Go wait at the campsite. I'll come back!" I said once again, and when I tried to take a step, my muscles spazzed, and I fell, landing on the floor with a hard thud. God fucking dammit.

I gotta make it back to the kitchen and see if she has anything I can stop this fucking bleeding with, and then I noticed at the end of the hallway there was a monitor that sprung to life where I can see everyone walking through their respective cabins. The only one who was limping was Fox, but she kept pushing.

Let's end this since I'm the one she wants. I took my knife from my pocket, stuck it in the wall, and used the handle to push myself up as best as I could. I evened my breathing and took one step at a time, deciding to shut off my pain altogether and make it to the kitchen.

I stopped in front of the lasers and used the end of my blade to reflect it on various parts of the room to spot the rest of the weapons.

One. Two. Three. Four. Since the moon was giving me plenty of light from the big ass window to the left of me, I could see the oven in the kitchen's time was 12:03AM. Good, that means the electricity is working.

"Are you okay!?" I heard a voice on the monitor say in front of me, and I shook my head yes, I don't need to worry them right now and solely focus on getting to the kitchen.

I said fuck it and decided to make a beeline for the kitchen, which was a poor decision on my part, but I don't care. Fuck this bitch, I ain't scared.

Thankfully I missed the majority of the bullets, but when I dove for the kitchen, and the shots kept popping off, I crawled and hid under the table for cover in case a bullet wanted to bounce off the wall or some shit.

I waited until all of them stopped firing, and eventually, they did. Good shit. Then I crawled back to the central part of the kitchen and looked under the sink for something to disinfect my wounds, and since it tore right through me and I was bleeding like a stuck pig, I had to move fast.

When I found a bottle of liquor, I double-checked it to make sure it wasn't laced or some shit cuz this bitch is really fucked up in the head and would do just about anything to win, so I used my match to check it, and it burned the right shade which let me know it was safe to use to disinfect my wound.

If I spend too much time thinking about how much this shit is gonna hurt, I'm not gonna want to do it, so I pulled up my blood-stained shirt, reached for my upper back, and dumped it until it ran down. The alcohol stung my throbbing wound, and I winced in pain, trying not to set off any more alarms in case there were any more left.

"I swear I'm gonna murder you when I get my fucking hands on you," I vowed in agony to myself. Then did the same to my leg, and I tried not to pass out from the pain that gripped my entire body.

I noticed since I had set off the majority of the lasers, they were gone, so I could now walk freely around the living room if I needed to, so I did all I could to stand up and limp towards the fireplace to grab an iron rod to close this goddamn wound and wrap it up as fast as I can. I have got to move, now.

Then an audio recording of our classmates screaming blared on the speakers, and I trembled with rage; Ooo, I'm gonna skin her ass alive. Now, this is psychological warfare she's declaring on us all.

"Kim, I know you're listening from a basement somewhere in this bitch, but I promise you when I find you, I will skin your ass alive, then hang you from the fucking trees until the flies, crows eat you whole," I promised. Then her laughter came over the intercom, "You talk a big game for someone whose bleeding and has been for the last couple of minutes."

"Flesh wound bitch, not that you would know," I answered.

She laughed some more, and it was empty, sadistic, and maniacal.

"Come try to stop me hoe, that's if you don't die or I don't kill the rest of your precious friends," She threatened.

"Fuck you!" I yelled, cauterizing my wound, then looked for something to cut my jeans and tie over my injuries so I could get back to moving. Goddamn, I'm all tore the fuck up, but I'm too pissed to think straight right now.

Then she played an audio recording of me fucking Nick in the woods, and I laughed, "You're sick, you know that," as the sounds of my moaning got louder in the house.

"What? I thought you wanted a pleasant memory before I kill all of you," She giggled.

"How thoughtful," I wryly smiled.

So I grabbed as many weapons as she was stupid enough to leave around and decided now would be a good time to look for the cell phones in the house. So I moved as fast as I could, ignoring the throbbing pain of my wounds and my muscles spazzing. Come the fuck on!

Before looking for our cell phones, I decided to take my gun and shoot down the rest of the miniguns in the house; I don't give a fuck if a bullet bounces off and hits me. I am too fucking angry right now.

Luckily I was able to destroy the majority of them and I heard her growl, which made me smile with satisfaction.

Then I found all of our cellphones and noticed it was only six, so that means she's been taking the cell phones of everyone that's dead so she can get rid of the evidence. Sneaky bitch.

I went back to the kitchen, got a ziplock bag, and tossed each of them in there, hoping one of them could turn on when I throw it out the door, hoping

Jasmine could see it when I do. That's if she's still alive. Please let her still be alive.

"Tess! I found her!" I heard Nick call out over the monitor near the entrance, "I hacked the mainframe, she's in the house where Fox is, but she's fucked up. I sent out the signal to call the cops, so they should be on the way. I'm leaving now! Meet you there! Please be safe." End reception. Shit gotta get out now.

I grabbed the bag with our cell phones and bolted for the doorway, but it was sealed shut. Fuck! Jasmine! If she's alive, she can open the door from the outside.

"JASMINE! JASMINE, PLEASE OPEN THE DOOR! I'M TRAPPED IN HERE!" I banged on it and waited for an answer.

"Tess?" She croaked, but barely, oh my God, she was bleeding this whole time? Oh shit!

"Jasmine, please open the door now, please!" I begged, "I can't feel my legs, but I'll try," She replied wearily. My stomach clenched, and my heart sank to the pits. Please open the damn door. I have to save as many as I can before my body gives out on me.

I heard a slow turn of the knob, and it swung open, but she was laying there lifeless with a pool of blood leaking from her leg shit.

I have to bandage her wound and stop the bleeding now, or she will die a slow, painful death. I tossed the ziplock bag with our phones over Jasmine's head until it landed in front of the walkway.

"Tess, I'm dizzy," she whispered, "I know, I'm coming back. Stay right there," I said.

Limping to grab the table that lined the hallway, I lifted and dragged it in front of the door to hold it open while I went back into the house and found something to wrap her wound with.

Come on, body, stop being a bitch! I thought when I involuntarily quivered by the time I dropped the table in front of the door.

MOVE NOW! Then bolted back to the kitchen to find a towel or something. When I did, I snatched it, the bottle of liquor, and used the last of my strength to run outside, then kick the table so the door would automatically shut on itself.

I fell to the ground huffing cuz my vision started to blur again, not now body, not fucking now.

"Stop being a bitch body and move," I ordered, grabbing the bottle of liquor, "Don't waste it on me. I'm gonna die here anyways."

"Shut up Jasmine, I promised myself if I can do something to save any of you, I'm going to. We need to hurry, Fox is banged up pretty bad and needs us all together," I reminded taking a large swig of it myself, then poured it over her bloody wound. She screamed in pain and passed out.

Good, now I can focus on stopping the bleeding. I tore the towel and tied it around her leg as tight as I could until she eventually stirred awake, "I'm alive?" She said in a daze.

"Yes, you're alive, now do me a favor, hold this bottle of liquor, I'm gonna take you to the main campsite where it's safe, the police are on the way, so I need you to hold on for a little while longer, can you do that for me?"

"I'll try," she said. Better than nothing.

I swallowed the searing pain that jolted up my spine when I lifted her dead weight from the ground, and I limped towards the center, gabbed the ziplock bag with our phones, and gave it to her, "Check to see if this has a signal or any battery okay?"

"Aren't you hurt?" She asked drowsily.

"Yes, but I can't think about that right now, so please focus and listen to me, see if any of these phones have power and if they do, turn one of them on, call the cops and let them know what's happening okay? Can you please do that? For me?"

"Okay," she replied, "Stay awake, do not go to sleep," I told her as a final warning.

Then took another deep breath and ran up the steps trying not to trip towards the house Fox went into, so when I met everyone else outside, all of them looked like they almost had a heart attack looking at me, "What the fuck happened?" Nick said, stunned.

"Oh my God! Are you fucking kidding me? How the fuck are you still moving?" Derek exclaimed.

"Now is not the time for that. Let's go, Fox is injured, and she needs us," I said but stumbled cuz my legs twitched, but Nessa caught me, "No, you stay out here," Nessa told me, "Fuck that! I'm gonna murder this bitch with my own two hands," I growled.

"You're only gonna slow the team down," Nessa reminded, "I won't; I've been through way worse than this," I reminded.

"Help me up," I told them, and they did, "Nessa, you go ahead, and find Fox, me, Nick, and Derek will look for her."

"Okay," She replied, and we all walked inside. Fox was lying on the living room floor unconscious, and Nessa lifted her from the ground and took her into the kitchen the same as I did. Thankfully cuz all of these houses are designed the same. It was something that became easy to rely on.

"Come on, lets go," I snapped trying to steady myself when I stood up, "How many bullets does that make?" Derek joked to lighten the mood.

"Four and a bear,"

"You're a bad bitch, and I wanna be like you when I grow up,"

"No, you don't cuz this shit hurts," I reminded.

"Found it," Nick said, and I followed after him, "Look, sharp guys."

I walked behind Nick, who aimed his gun around, and when we made it downstairs to the fortified bunker, I was the first to find her where she was glaring directly at me with a maniacal smile on her lips in the dark with screens as far as the eye could see. So she was watching us the entire time. I fucking knew it.

"No, you know what, I'm not gonna shoot you. You deserve so much worse than that," I hissed.

Then the rest I don't remember what happened after, all I know is when I came back I felt someone pulling me off of her, "Get off of me! She's the one who put everyone through this fucked up shit, to begin with!" I rumbled swinging like a mad woman not realizing I had reopened my wounds and more blood had covered my body.

I couldn't feel a damn thing cuz yet again, I was too enraged to feel pain.

"Why did you do this?" Derek snapped, and I heard her laugh, "because I can, and you monkeys needed to be reminded whose in charge, and it damn sure isn't you like my mother wanted to in the first place,"

"Did you kill her?" Nick demanded to know, "Yes, I did, so what?" She said, and the room fell silent as they both turned to look back at me in shock.

"I couldn't stand the thought of my mother trying to unite us all as one school to try and change the idea that poor niggers and rich white kids like myself. So I came up with a little game to see whose the stronger race because I CAN and its MY school. Not hers and damn sure isn't my fathers," She laughed, finally showing her true colors.

I started to shake again when my blood ran hot with rage needing to cave her skull in with my bare hands.

"So you were faking the whole time to be my friend!?" Derek screeched in disbelief, "I would never actually be friends with someone who's both ugly and beneath me. How fucking stupid can you be?! Oh wait, that's right, you wanted someone to love you SO bad that you ran to me and told me all about how your parents locked you in a wooden box cuz you like both men and women. Give me a fucking break, you pussy," She said; even though her face is all bruised and bloody, she still has the nerve to talk shit.

"Let go of me, Nick, so I can beat this bitches ass to death myself," I said through grit teeth, "and poor Nick needing to be the man so damn bad he has to sell drugs to make ends meet, and you too came running to me for some money right? Pathetic. All of you disgust me,"

"NICK, I'M ASKING YOU TO LET ME GO AND MURDER THIS BITCH!"

"Nah, cuz I got something even better," He said cooly.

"Check the monitor," He said, and when Kim turned around, I noticed it said record in our room.

She was stupid enough to have a camera in her own room and Nick had been recording this entire conversation.

"YOU FILTHY FUCKING NIGGER HOW DARE YOU!"

"So the secrets out, and you're going to jail for a really long time, and last time I checked, orange jumpsuits are not in this season," He boasted with a chuckle.

"Well, that means my ass is going to jail too for assault and attempted murder, but I'm cool with it," I laughed with joy, "Cuz that means you're coming down with me, you vile fucking creature," I said.

On one of the cameras, the police had finally shown up and stormed each house until they found and arrested all of us, including Kim.

Victory is mine bitch. I win this game.

We won.

When they brought us all down to the station and found ashes of our classmates had been incinerated, we told them the truth about Kim, and thankfully cuz she was stupid enough to keep the waivers everyone signed that specifically said at the bottom, you forfeit your life by accepting to come on this trip in teeny-tiny print.

And me? Well, I'm going to the hospital first, then to jail, but I damn sure don't mind. Cuz truthfully, all of us are going for murder. We didn't bother with a trial, but no matter what happened from then on out, we were all together and lived out our sentence.

Ironically since everyone heard about us, we had earned respect and I ran into people I never thought I would've seen again, people from my past and that meant I wasn't the only one who was safe inside, my friends were too.

And yeah, me and Nick are officially dating, can't say I saw that one coming, but at the end of it all, our bond was tighter than ever, and while Jasmine still complains about everything, it became something we all joked about.

We also joked about how Derek can find a boyfriend in here, and we all laughed about it. Fox wrote a helluva lot in her cell and shared her writing and poetry with us, and most times it left us in awe, and Nessa finished her sentence by doing extra curricular stuff.

Once she got out, we all did the same, which shortened our sentence.

When we all got out, I did my best to live my life not just for the people I've lost, but even for the people whose lives I've ended, we all aren't perfect, but I can say I don't live in fear of anything anymore.

I realized the reason why Kim was so adamant to stay in power and use our own fears against us is that she was more afraid of us than we were of her.

Her beliefs of how the world should be was the real reason why she did everything she did. It's why she created the entire system and used our different backgrounds and beliefs against each other, which is why we mistrusted the other.

She caused our division by those beliefs we held onto so firmly for dear life until we were at each other's throats, which ultimately led to death and the bloodshed in this entire story.

It wasn't until I faced myself with Nick by my side that I could spend some time with myself and my own sins, personal beliefs and even start questioning things like I used to a long time ago. So the real culprit in this entire thing is our own fears.

Its why we mistrust each other, and it causes our division in front of the imminent enemy and now people are dead because of our fears. Even mine.

But the more time I spent with myself, looking for peace and challenging my own beliefs, I cried a whole lot, and by the time I left, I was finally free of my own fears, and since we stayed tight after everything, so were they.

Don't miss out!

Visit the website below and you can sign up to receive emails whenever Kornelia Blackmore publishes a new book. There's no charge and no obligation.

https://books2read.com/r/B-A-GOZN-RIGSB

BOOKS 2 READ

Connecting independent readers to independent writers.

Did you love *The Blood Covenant: Mistrust, Division, & Murder*? Then you should read *Truth & Dare*[1] by Kornelia Blackmore!

College students, Yumi, Ares, & Phoebe invite Yumi's ex bf Caleb on a camping trip (who were friends in high school.)

But when a game of Truth & Dare is proposed around the bonfire by Ares, what secrets are revealed?

Read more at www.twitter.com/kblackmore26362.

1. https://books2read.com/u/brwODZ

2. https://books2read.com/u/brwODZ

Also by Kornelia Blackmore

Crowning
The Blood Covenant: Mistrust, Division, & Murder
Truth & Dare

Watch for more at www.twitter.com/kblackmore26362.

About the Author

I started my writing journey as an angsty teenager back in 2008, and I noticed how many reviews I kept getting for the fan fictions I wrote on their website over the years. One day I was reading a Webtoon by June Purr called SubZero and intrigued with the idea of wanting to create a world but with people of color, that's what birthed Kornelia Blackmore.

Normally this is the part where I tell you I have degrees but I don't Just another really cool mini story that set me on the path in my early college years.

I failed my English composition classes (and even creative writing). Until I came across a really cool guy named Mr. D at Prince Georges Community College.

He was one of the first people to have ever made me feel like I was a writer, and even asked me "how the hell did you end up in my class?" until eventually everyone in my class was asking me for help with their writing pieces. I think that was probably the only other time in life I felt accomplished from others asking me for help, and I grew to love the experience as a means to solidify my place as an artist.

But, writing is my lifeblood, and this is the quote I live by in all of my writing projects;

"Life has enough limitations. Writing shouldn't be one of them."

This quote is how I aspire to learn the art of writing in all its different forms and genres and will continue to pursue that passion with the same dedication in everything else I do.

I would rather you guys get to know me, as me, instead of some stuffy long biography that no one ever really reads. But thank you for buying my book, and reading it.

Blessings friends.

Read more at www.twitter.com/kblackmore26362.